Anchored Hearts Vol. 2.5

Fading Away

International Bestselling Author

J.M. WITT

Acknowledgments

Rick: Nice try! Telling my fans that everyone dies. Not *everyone* dies. Geesh!

D, A, E, T: I hope one day you understand why Mommy spends so much time on the laptop. My hard work isn't only for me, but for you, too!

To my friends: Keep reading and spreading the word. I'm forever grateful to you!

Betsy: Thank you for putting up with me. It's a relief knowing that I can come to you, anytime, and you're ready to help, listen, plot, etc.

The Betas: Rebecca, Tracey, Elaine, Tami, Betsy, Melanie, Letty, Jessica, and Lisa. Thank you. I know I was pushing the deadline on this one and you came through for me. I'll try not to make a habit out of it!

Letty and Jessica: You saved this book! I hate commas, clearly. Lol. Heart you hard!

Anchored Hearts ST: Without your support, I wouldn't be where I am. Love you, girls!

Tyf: It's true, we share a brain. Thank you for ALWAYS being there for me. You know how to make me laugh and I know I can lean on you when needed.

Skye: I love you long time. You know why. Thank you.

Fading Away

one

I NEARLY JUMPED OUT OF MY SKIN when I felt a hand soothing my back. Looking up I found James staring back at me. He looked like he had been crying and the sight of it ripped the hole in me even bigger. I started hyperventilating. He let me cry my fill and didn't say a word.

"It's all my fault. I should've said yes, I wanted to say yes. But I-I r-ran instead." James just consoled me and let me get out what I needed to. "I can't make it w-without him, James. I just c-can't. It hurts, it hurts so much. Please make it stop."

He placed his hands on my shoulders and pushed me an arm's length away. "Jane, you need to relax, you're both going to be fine."

Shaking his hands off me I stood and stepped away from him. "I'm not going to be f-fine. The love of my life is d-dead, he's dead, and it's all because of me."

"Jane, Cal isn't dead." He stood then and pulled me off the bench.

"Yes he is. I saw the doctors pull his family into the grieving room and so did you. He's g-gone and I'm the one who killed him." James was looking at me like he was contemplating what I had said as I kept rambling. "It's just like with Jason. I kept quiet about the drug use too long. If I'd told mom and dad maybe he'd still be here. If I'd just told Calvin about Derek this wouldn't have happened. Cal would've protected me, been prepared."

"Jane, Calvin made it through surgery."

"But, I…the resident said to prepare for the worst."

"Jane, he made it. He's in really rough shape, but he made it. They said the next twenty four hours will be the most critical."

I took a couple deep breaths trying to process his words as my chin began to tremble. Burying my face in my hands I burst into obnoxious sobs like a simpering child. Years of fear, regret, hurt, and loss racked their way through my body. When I got it together, barely, I pulled away from James and wiped the tears from my face.

"I have to see him."

James grabbed my hand and led the way up to ICU. We were at the desk, fighting with the nurse to see Cal, when I saw Cassidy step out of a room. She spotted us instantly and I saw the relief wash over her at the sight of James. She rushed over to us as we ignored the nurse's protests about the number of visitors allowed.

We sat down in an adjoining waiting room and Cassidy filled us in as best she could. He was on a ventilator, but they were hopeful he'd be off of it soon, if he made it through the next twenty four hours. It was a miracle alone that Cal had pulled through surgery.

"Can I see him?"

"Yes, I'll put you on the list. They're monitoring him closely, but it shouldn't be a problem."

I knew the strict policy the hospital had, especially for ICU. Family only and any other visitors had to be approved by the family. After Cassidy talked to the front desk, I made my way into his room. I'd seen this scenario a dozen times, doing several rotations in the trauma unit and ICU floors, during nursing school. But I wasn't prepared to see Cal that way. He was extremely pale, IVs coming out of both arms and machines beeping their own familiar rhythms.

The weight of the day's events suddenly dropped on my shoulders like a ton of bricks. It was all I could do to stand any longer. I pulled a chair to the side of his bed and collapsed in it. The faint rays of dawn were becoming visible through the closed blinds. Placing his hand in mine, I dropped my head to the bed.

When I woke, I realized I had been asleep for several hours. I glanced around the room to find Dave asleep in a chair by the door. Cal looked the same. I heard the door open and turned to see a familiar face. Her name was Jessica and we'd gone through nursing school together. We weren't close during nursing school, but we got along fine.

"I heard you were back in town." She smiled sweetly before changing out an IV bag and checking the routine things she was supposed to.

"You heard right. How long have you been up here?" Last I had heard she was working in the ER.

"A couple years now. You still working in NICU?"

I nodded. "Been back upstairs for about six weeks now." I ran my hands over my face and was instantly reminded of the swelling and injuries to my face. I could only imagine how I looked to her.

"You don't have to work tonight do you? Looks like you could use some rest too."

"Sylvia gave me the week off and told me to keep her posted." Dave started to rouse and we both quieted down.

Whispering she asked, "Who's the hottie?" She motioned toward

Cal and I couldn't help but smile. "I wouldn't have pictured you with, well…"

"A tatted up cop? You and me both. He's incredible." My voice grew shaky as I brought my hand to my mouth to try to get myself under control. She came over and rubbed a hand on my shoulder.

"He did really well through the night, better than we could've hoped or expected. I'll be here to keep an eye on him for the rest of the day. You should go home and get some rest and something to eat."

"I don't know. They said that the first twenty four hours were the most critical. I'd never forgive myself if something happened and I wasn't here."

"Jane, you got a strong one there. If he's as incredible as you say he is, he'd want you to take care of yourself. You've been through a trauma too."

Sniffing, "Ok, I know you're right. Can you please call or text me if there's any change?"

"Sure, what's your number?"

I searched in my pockets, so I could store her number in my phone, and realized I didn't have my purse, phone or anything with me. After giving Jessica my number I headed to the elevators.

As the doors opened, I saw Cassidy and James staring back at me. James took in my appearance as Cassidy asked if everything was ok with Cal. I assured her Cal was as good as to be expected, that I was just exhausted. I asked if I could borrow James for a moment. He kissed Cassidy on the forehead before she walked toward Cal's room.

"Jane, what's going on?"

"I'm just wrecked. I need to go home. Did you get a hold of mom and dad yet?" Mom and Dad had already flown out when all the chaos commenced the day prior.

"They're flying back and should be home later tonight or tomorrow. I can drive you. Where do you want me to take you?"

"Um, I…I don't know where my purse or phone are. My keys are in there."

He reached in his pocket and handed me my phone. "You left it at my parents place along with your purse. It's in my truck. But your car is still at your parents. We got Cal's truck back home this morning. I can drop you off at your place, so you can rest, and I'll get Smith to help me get your car back to you by this evening."

"Thank you. Ok. I don't think I can go to mom and dad's right now, not with what happened."

As he drove me back to Cal's I dozed off. When I woke up, we were pulling in the drive. My heart began to race and my hands grew sweaty. I didn't want to be alone at Cal's. "Will you come in with me?" It was *our* place now, had been for a while and I needed to get that through my head. He was willing to die for me and me for him.

James looked to me, "I'm such an idiot. Of course."

I handed him the keys out of my purse and he opened the door. It felt so foreign walking into our place without Cal. I lived there, but would he still want me when he woke up? If he woke up? James seemed to understand my trepidation and searched the place before he gave me the all clear.

"Is there anything I can get you?"

I shook my head, "No. I just want to sleep."

"I'll be here."

Nodding, I walked up the stairs to our room. Starting to undress, I had planned to take a shower, but couldn't resist sitting on the bed. I looked at the clock on the bedside table and saw it was already late afternoon. Grabbing his pillow, I buried my face in it and laid down. His scent was there and I fell asleep with his aroma floating above me like a halo.

When I woke, I was incredibly sore. My whole body ached and in places I didn't want to think about. I rolled over realizing my shoes were off and a blanket was covering me. I was shocked at the time. Had a whole day really passed? My cell phone was on the nightstand, on the charger and it verified that I had indeed slept for almost twenty four hours.

I began to panic. I leapt out of bed faster than my body wanted me to and cursed myself as the aches seared my body. Frantically I pulled on some jeans and checked my phone again. All the missed calls from Cal, James and Derek, from two days ago, were there, along with several missed texts. There was one I didn't recognize and I opened it immediately.

It was from Jessica. According to the time stamp, she sent it at the end of her shift last night. I swore my heart almost stopped as I read her words. Relief flooded me as I digested her text. Cal was doing well, but he was still unconscious and on the vent.

Hurrying down the stairs, I found James on the couch scrolling through his phone.

"You're finally awake. How are you feeling?"

"I'm ok. You should've woken me. Is he ok? Is there any word."

"Calm down. There's been no change. If something had changed I would've woken you. You needed rest." I ran my hands through my hair, not sure what to do first. "Hey. He's going to be fine. Go take a shower and I'll make you something to eat and then we can head to the hospital."

"Ok. Thank you." I hugged him before making my way back upstairs.

Stepping into the bathroom, I looked at my reflection and took a shaky breath as my eyes met my image in the mirror. I removed the bandage, revealing my swollen and bruised left eye, from which I could barely see, and examined the stitches. I jumped as the gunshot rang through the air of my memory. Derek was gone. James had killed him. I wouldn't have to worry about Derek any longer. Cal was my only concern.

James. How was he handling killing a man? I had to make sure he was ok and that the cops knew it was self-defense. I let the water run over me as I tried to hurry and be mindful of my injuries. The water ran red for a short time as I worked the matted blood out of my hair.

When I had dressed and made my way downstairs, James was on his phone. The smell of food filled the air and my ravenous stomach took over. He'd made grilled cheese and tomato soup, one of my favorite quick and easy meals. I took a bite out of a sandwich as I found a thermos to pour the soup in. I wasn't going to hang out at home any longer. I had to get to Cal.

"Jane, I hate to do this, but I have to run to the office. Will you be ok driving?"

"It's ok. Thank you for everything you've done for me. I should be able to manage."

"Your mom and dad are back. They're headed to the hospital and will meet you there."

"Ok. James. What you did? How did you know?"

"I had a bad feeling, Jane. Honestly, I spotted your cell and started snooping. We don't need to talk about it."

He tried to turn away, but I grabbed his forearm. "James, you killed a man for me and if I had been honest with everyone from the beginning…Well, I'm sorry."

"Jane, you don't have anything to be sorry for. But there's something you need to know."

My eyes narrowed at him as I shook my head, "What is it?"

"Derek's alive." I didn't hear anything else he said as fear slammed into me. I couldn't breathe and the room began to spin. "Jane, sit down. He won't hurt you anymore. He's in a coma and cuffed to the bed as a precaution. Jane?" I just nodded as he pulled me close. "I promise you. He will not hurt you anymore. I'll make sure of it." As much as I wanted Derek dead, I didn't want James to live with the guilt of it.

A few minutes later we were standing outside as I climbed into my car. "James, I'll be fine. I'll text you when I get there."

"Alright. I'll see you soon." He closed my door as I started the engine and he got in his truck and drove away.

I called Cassidy before I made my way to the hospital and apologized profusely for missing so much, explaining that I'd fallen asleep. She understood and after getting orders from everyone, I picked up coffee and snacks on the way.

I situated the coffee in my passenger seat and then myself in the driver's seat, but couldn't stand the silence or my thoughts running amock in my head any longer. I pushed play on my iPod and continued to hit 'next' until I found something I wanted to hear. I stopped on *Running Up That Hill* by Placebo.

I replayed it over and over, louder than necessary, the entire drive to the hospital. The tears ran down my cheeks, but the sobs were long gone. For the time being, anyway. I'd have given anything to trade places with Cal. I was the one who should have been laying in that hospital bed, not him.

Walking into his hospital room, I found Dave and Cassidy chatting quietly before they spotted me. I handed them their coffee and a bag of pastries which they were grateful for.

"You look so much better." Dave was teasing me, while also being sincere.

"What are you trying to say?" I was genuinely feeling better, but still very sore. I'd removed the bandage on my eye and replaced it with a smaller one, though the bruises looked worse now than they did two days ago. "Any new updates?" I noticed the ventilator was still in place, Cal still not awake.

"The doctors aren't sure when he'll wake up. They say it's just a matter of time."

"But everything looks normal?" Cassidy and Dave nodded before saying their goodbyes. They had stayed with him all night and day and were headed back to Cassidy's place to shower and rest. I took my position next to his bedside and placed his hand in mine.

I was playing with his fingers, memorizing every line, callus, and knuckle when I felt a hand on my shoulder. I looked to see that my mom and dad had arrived. I wasn't sure how long they'd been there watching me as I watched Cal.

Standing, I hugged her and she held on a little longer than usual, but I couldn't blame her. "Mom, I'm alright. I'm going to be ok, as long as he pulls through, I'll be just fine."

"I love you, Jane."

"I love you too, Mom." She released me and Dad then pulled me to him.

"Janey, I don't know what we'd do without you."

"I'm sorry." My voice cracked as the tears came again. I was embarrassed and ashamed, knowing I shouldn't have been.

"Don't be. I'm sorry we didn't pick up on all the signs." Dad kissed my head as he said, "I blame myself. I've spent too long on the road and away from my girls."

"Dad, this isn't your fault. Derek had us all fooled. I never thought he'd go to such extremes."

"Alright you two. That's enough." Dad released me, but I stayed burrowed into his side. "I'm hungry. Do you want to come to the cafeteria with us, or can we bring you something back?"

"No. I'm good. Well, maybe some snacks and some caffeine would be nice to get me through the night."

Once they left, a nurse came in to check Cal's vitals. Nothing had changed and I turned the TV on to help pass the time.

two

Christmas Eve
~ JANE ~

A DAY LATER WE WERE STILL WAITING for Cal to wake up. Cassidy or Dave always sat with him during the day and I took the night shifts. I had to go back to work in a couple of days and I wasn't sure how I'd handle it if he was still unconscious.

They removed the breathing tube that day, which was a good sign, but not good enough for me. I was starting to see the change in his body, too. He was losing weight and it was becoming noticeable. He worked out almost every day and he wouldn't be happy about the muscle he was losing.

I was trying to remain optimistic, but every hour made it harder. The doctors couldn't offer any advice, just kept saying that he should wake up any day. I needed him to pull through, I needed him.

Why had it taken me so long to realize that?

Christmas morning we gathered together, all praying for our Christmas miracle. But, he didn't wake up. I had to return to work and began promising Cal anything and everything if he'd just wake up. But it didn't happen. My medical background was becoming a curse. I knew the longer he remained in a coma the more likely he was to remain there.

The next evening, I stopped into his room before my shift. Cassidy was heading out and we hugged. Neither of us spoke as we stood at the end of his bed, willing him to wake. I squeezed her hand and looked to her as the tears fell down both our faces. Shortly thereafter, she left and I sat down in the bedside chair.

People say what doesn't kill you makes you stronger. The stress, hurt, anxiety, pressure, and the other things I had lost felt worse than death possibly could. But I couldn't lose him. I was feeling hopeless, for the place I was at in life, and I knew it would either make me or break me.

Well, it couldn't break what was already broken. I was broken and learning to accept that I would probably never be whole again, and that was ok, as long as I had Cal. When he was next to me, the strength I felt was almost enough to make me feel whole once more, if even for just a moment. But he *had* to wake up.

My shift that night was uneventful and I got off at my scheduled time and headed straight for his room. He was laying there, like he had been for almost a week. Appearing to be asleep, like nothing was wrong.

My eye was looking much better and my body wasn't as sore as it had been, but I was exhausted. Sleep had been restless for me and filled with nightmares. I pulled the chair next to his bed and laid my head down next to him as I held his hand. It was the only place I wanted to be.

I was dreaming of Cal stroking my hair, imagining how good it felt. We were lying in bed, tangled in one another while drawing lazy circles on each other with our fingers. I didn't want to wake from the dream, but knew I needed to.

I didn't move as I let my eyes adjust to the room. I realized that I wasn't holding his hand anymore and someone *was* playing with my hair. My mind had to be playing tricks on me as I stared at the closed door to his hospital room. I couldn't bear to look at his sleeping face anymore. I wanted to scream at him, and would have if I thought he'd wake up sooner.

Slowly, I pulled my head up just enough to turn my eyes toward his face. His eyes were looking right at me and he was smiling sweetly. I was losing my mind. Bringing my hands up to my eyes, I rubbed them vigorously. I dropped my head in my hands trying to shake off the misery.

"Baby doll." It was barely audible.

I bolted upright, rubbing my eyes again before I looked at him.

"Cal, you're awake! How long have you been awake?"

His voice was hoarse as he croaked out, "Just a few minutes."

I felt the tears falling down my cheeks as I leaned down to kiss him. I cupped his face as I placed kisses all over his whiskers, his eyes, his nose, and forehead.

"I need to call your doctor." I went to pull away and he squeezed my hand as tight as he could, and his expression turned into one of concern.

"Jane, are you ok? Your face? The last thing I remember…"

"I'm ok. I'll fill you in, but not right now." He still looked very grim. "Cal, I promise I'm ok. I'm more than ok. You came back to me and now I have a chance to make things right."

"How long have I been out?"

"Almost a week."

"Jesus." I gave him a quick peck before walking briskly to the nurses' station.

About an hour later Cal was sound asleep after several doctors looked him over and checked out various things. They were going to run some tests, but the only thing concerning Cal had been when he could go home. We all told him not to push it, that it would probably be a week or two. He was determined it wouldn't be longer than a week.

I called Cassidy and Dave to let them know he was awake. Cassidy stopped by after work and we embraced and observed as more doctors fawned over him. The relief was evident in her body language, like you could see the weight lifted off her shoulders, but she still seemed sad.

"Cassidy, is everything else ok?" Something else was bothering her. The girl's emotions were always written all over her face.

"Oh it's nothing, I'm sure. It's just, I'm just worried about James." She was shifting nervously from one foot to the other.

"What's going on?"

In all the chaos over the past week, I'd never even had a chance to really talk to James about everything that happened like I had planned. He was taken in for questioning, but quickly released given the circumstances. He shot another man and not in battle, and I knew he wouldn't be ok with that. I started to become anxious for him and I didn't even know if or what Cassidy knew about his military past and how tumultuous it had been. Who was I kidding? I didn't know how tumultuous it had been either.

"He's just been really distant. I know he's spending a lot of time with his mom, and I don't fault him for that, but, there's just something else going on."

"He'll be ok. He's been through a lot. Don't worry. Be patient and try to talk to him about it." I smiled and she returned it with a smile of her own. Before they left the room, the doctors reminded us about how exhausted Cal would be during his recovery. I gave Cassidy a few minutes with Cal, knowing she needed some time with him.

I was in the lobby when Dave showed up. He hugged me so vigorously, my feet were swept off the ground. We spent a few hours together watching Cal as he drifted in and out of sleep. James never showed up and I didn't think anything of it until Dave and Cassidy left.

Early the next morning I walked into his room to find a food tray with empty containers. My shift had been extremely busy, which I was grateful for because I had been utterly exhausted. Nothing like several crying newborns to wake you up.

Cal's nurses told me he'd slept most of the night, but had managed to find time to eat. The fact that he was eating was a great sign. Walking to his bedside I grazed my hand over his forehead and into his hair and he began to stir. His eyes fluttered open and he smiled at me.

"Sorry, I didn't mean to wake you."

"Rather you than that old bag trying to cop a feel. She's been threatening to give me a sponge bath all night. I'd rather *you* give me a bath." He flashed those dimples and tried grabbing my ass. He was definitely feeling better.

I couldn't help but burst into laughter. He must have been referring to Gladys who was his night nurse's aide. Her bawdiness rivaled my mother's. Her and I had some pretty funny conversations about Cal, mostly one sided, about her talking of what she'd do with him given the opportunity. She also didn't shy away from flirting with his dad, Dave, who played right along with her. Clearly the apple hadn't fallen far from the tree.

"Oh come on. She's a sweet lady just looking for some fun." I winked at him, "I think I'll see if she can squeeze that bath in before her shift ends."

He grabbed my wrist before I could walk to the door and pulled me down to him. "The only one bathing me is you!" I giggled into his mouth as he kissed me, happy that his sense of humor was still intact. I helped him sit up and then sat on the end of the bed facing him.

Reaching my hands under the covers I started massaging his calves. It dawned on me that we hadn't had more than a few minutes to ourselves since he woke. I was worried about overstepping my bounds, but wanted to hold him so badly. We sat staring and smiling at one another for a little while before he broke the silence.

"We need to talk, Jane."

Oh, shit. Here it comes. I smiled sweetly and waited for him to start talking. We did need to talk.

~ CALVIN ~

I'D NEVER BEEN so happy to see her eyes staring into mine. On the outside she seemed perfectly fine, minus her bruised and scraped face, but I had figured out beforehand that she was a master of hiding her emotions. Even then, she was smiling at me like she didn't have a care in the world.

"What happened with Derek?" She just stared at me as the wheels in her head turned. "Jane, I don't remember much of anything except walking into your room and Derek pointing a gun at me." She just stared at me as I continued, "I gather he shot me, but what happened before, after?"

"Um, James showed up with a gun. After you...and James shot him."

"Christ. Is he dead?" She just shook her head. "Jail?"

"He's in the hospital, in a coma, too. James didn't have a choice, Derek was about to shoot me so James shot him."

How could she have been involved with someone like him? "Jane, you were involved with this guy? Did you suspect he was…" The look on her face told me that she was hiding something. "Tell me!"

"I didn't think, well, that he'd do anything so crazy. He'd been calling me and I thought I saw him the night we got the Christmas tree…"

"WHAT? Jane, I need to know these things." I was infuriated and my chest began radiating with pain. "Fuck."

"Cal, you need to calm down."

Machines started beeping and my nurse came running in almost immediately. "What's going on guys? Calvin? You need to relax." The nurse, Jessica, grabbed my wrist as she kept an eye on her watch. "You can't be getting worked up. I need you to take some deep breaths and close your eyes."

I drifted off a few minutes later and didn't wake up until late in the day. Jane left me a note saying she'd stop in before her shift to see me.

Cassidy spent several hours at the hospital with me before Dad took her home. She was worried about James and I wasn't sure what to tell her. I was beginning to wonder if he was suffering from some form of PTSD. When we had talked a month prior I had gotten the feeling that he'd been through some rough times during his time in the Army, but he also mentioned that Cassidy hadn't known he'd served. I had to ask her.

"Cassidy, has he told you about his time in the service?"

"What? You know? Why does everyone know but me?"

"Cassidy, you need to talk to him, but go easy. Not every vet likes to discuss their time in the service."

"Smith let it slip. He has nightmares, but he never talks to me about them."

THE REST OF the day had passed uneventfully. Jessica and an orderly helped me walk to the bathroom. I was confident I wouldn't need their help, but was wrong when my legs wouldn't work properly. It was humiliating.

"You're doing great. You've been immobile for over a week. It's ok." Jessica was a great nurse and it helped she was friendly with Jane.

Jane stopped in before her shift and at my insistence climbed into bed with me. She was exhausted and needed some rest if she was going to function at work. Early in the evening, Cassidy stopped by again with James in tow. Jane was burrowed into my side, fast asleep. I waved them over, but put my finger to my lips requesting they keep quiet.

I outstretched my free hand to James saying, "Good to see you, man."

"Same here. You doing okay?"

"As good as can be expected. I'll be happy when I can get out of here."

"Knock it off. You're not going anywhere until the doctors assure us you're in the clear." My sister was being a nag and James was getting a kick out of it.

"Have they said when they think you can go home?"

"They said a couple weeks, but I'm determined for it to be sooner."

Jane woke up, like she knew I was contemplating my escape, scolding me, "Let the doctors and nurses take care of you. There's no rush for you to get home."

"Hush, woman." I showed her my dimples before crushing my lips to hers.

"You hush!"

Jane got off the bed and took James in the hall, giving Cass and me a few minutes alone.

"You sure you're feeling ok?"

"Cass, I'm feeling great. Sore and tired, but I'm good. How are you?" Motioning my head toward the hall, "How's he?"

"I don't know. We haven't really had a chance to talk about everything. There's a lot going on with Dan and Melissa."

"What do you mean?"

"I don't know. But she's around a lot and I don't like it."

I had a feeling she was holding back and I didn't have the energy to press her further. I knew James was watching out for her and I had to have faith he would continue to do so. Jane and James walked back in at that time.

"James, I owe you my life. Thank you." He seemed surprised at my words as he looked to me as if my thanks wasn't necessary. "Jane told me what you did for us. I can't thank you enough."

"It's not necessary. You'd do the same for me." We shook hands as he told me to get some rest. Cass had a big smile on her face as they left.

three

New Year's Eve
~ CALVIN ~

FRANK HAD STOPPED BY THAT afternoon and he filled me in that Derek had awoken. I was livid and itching to get my hands on him.

"Just give me five minutes, alone, with him."

"I understand brother. If I could, I would. He's got a guard on him 24/7 and everybody knows what he did to Jane. They won't let you in to see him for *your* own good."

"Fuck!" I threw the breathing contraption they'd given me across the room. The memory of Jane being held as his shield, bloodied and bruised, had me seeing red. We still hadn't really had a chance to talk. She had assured me she was ok, but we *had* to talk about it. We'd never recover properly if we didn't.

Cass stopped in that night with cupcakes and other goodies as we waited for James to show up. The later it got, I could tell she was becoming furious, while I was exhausted. If I was going to make it to midnight I needed to get some rest.

Jane said the words before I could. "Do you want to go grab dinner down in the cafeteria, Cassidy?"

"What? Oh, umm."

"Cass, go have dinner with Jane. I need to get a little rest if you two are insisting on watching the ball drop tonight."

"Yeah, okay. If James shows up just tell him we'll be back."

I checked my cell after they left and had a missed call from Paul. He'd left a voicemail and was planning to stop by later in the night. I debated about when and what I should tell Cassidy about Paul being back in town. It wasn't like they had some tumultuous love affair, besides she was with James. I fell asleep before I had any longer to contemplate it.

~ JANE ~

"So, what's going on with my brooding cousin?"

"Brooding, you got that right." We laughed. "He's been really off the last few weeks, especially since the shooting." She caught the cringe that crossed my face and apologized. "Sorry. I know it must be difficult for you, especially with Derek alive."

"It's ok. I have to talk about it at some point. He's cuffed to the bed with a guard watching him and once he's stable enough they'll transport him to county. I know he can't hurt me anymore."

"Does Cal know?"

"That Derek is alive? Yeah. I told him earlier. He's happy that he's alive so that James doesn't have to live with the guilt of killing a man."

She seemed to be mulling something over before she asked me, "Do you know anything about his time in the Army?"

"Not really. He never really talked about it and I never asked. If he wants to talk about something he will."

"Mmm. He never told me he served. Smith let it slip."

Taking a sip of my drink, I processed her words. "I'm surprised and not surprised that he hasn't told you. He was wounded in a pretty bad ambush. He lost almost half of his platoon."

"Oh, my God. I had no idea." She was quiet for a moment before she started to ask me another question. "What..." But she was interrupted by her phone. She scanned it for a moment, a text message I presumed and tossed it back in her purse.

"That him?"

"How'd you guess? He's running *late*."

"You okay?" She nodded, but I knew she wasn't.

"I just wish he'd open up. I want to know every part of him, good and bad."

I forced a grin and said, "You and your brother are so much alike. James and I grew up in a loving family, but emotions, at least sad ones, weren't well received. You and Cal welcome *all* emotions with open arms. It's refreshing. But you may have to decide if you can handle him being shut off. And he may open up in time. You need to pick your battles."

I tried giving her the best advice I could. We all knew I wasn't one to tell my own secrets and I certainly wasn't about to spill any more of James'. We caught up on the other things going on in our lives while we finished dinner.

We headed back up to Cal's room and found him climbing back in bed. It was great to see him up and walking around, but it was obvious that he wasn't at full strength.

We sat around for another hour or so when Cassidy stood up and put her coat on. "Alright lovebirds. I think I'm going to head home."

"No, you should stay."

"Cass, please stay. Ring in the new year with us." Cal looked concerned, but Cassidy ignored it. She was irritated and I couldn't blame her.

"No. You two should be alone. Enjoy the cupcakes. They're your favorite. I'll stop in tomorrow to visit." She kissed Cal on the cheek and gave him a big hug before leaving.

I got off the bed after Cassidy left and Cal asked me, "Where do you think you're going?"

I smiled and replied, "Meddling. I'll be back in a few minutes." He pouted at me to which I laughed. "Don't. I'm calling James. I'll be right back." I blew him a kiss before I scampered out the door.

I made my way downstairs and tried calling James—twice—and both times I went to voicemail. I left him a message and then sent him a text. I was beginning to worry that something was seriously wrong with him. He was head over heels for Cassidy. Why was he keeping her at arm's length?

Before heading back to Cal's room I ran up to my floor to get my work schedule for the week. When I returned Cal told me that I had just missed his buddy Paul.

"He could've stayed."

"I told him to get out since it looked like it was just going to be you and me tonight." He waggled his brows at me. "You're ridiculous! Dream on Officer Charles."

We were curled up on the bed, flipping back and forth between the different New Year's Eve broadcasts, when James barged in. He was scanning the room and I knew he was looking for Cassidy.

"Hey guys. Where's Cassidy?"

I climbed off the bed and walked to stand in front of him. "She left over an hour ago." James looked to me as I furrowed my brow at him. "What are you doing, James?"

Ignoring me, he asked, "Who took her home?"

"I assume she left alone."

Cal immediately perked up. "What's going on?"

"Shit."

"Don't make me get out of this hospital bed, James." Cal continued, "My sister's pissed with you. I thought I warned you about her temper?" Cal was on the verge of laughing, but I knew James didn't find it funny. "Are you a glutton for punishment?"

James started pacing as he raked his hands over his face. "Dammit. She was attacked a couple days before the Christmas party. I've had a bodyguard on her since then. Damn her."

Cal bolted upright in the bed. "What do you mean she was attacked? You better spill it right now, Benedict."

Benedict? That was the first I'd heard Cal refer to James that way. It was somehow fitting. "Cal, calm down. I'm sure it's a misunderstanding." I turned to James, "What's going on?"

He sat down and said, "It's not a misunderstanding." He pulled out his cell and made a call. After hanging up he said, "She's home. Smith is sending Ryan over to watch her place until I can get there."

"I'm still waiting." Cal was about to burst a blood vessel in his forehead.

James explained everything that had been going on. It was no wonder he'd been emotionally distant. He was in protector mode, for Cassidy and me both. He never was good at separating the two roles.

Cal and James debated a few things, but agreed that it was most likely Dan who was behind everything. And as much as we all hated it, if Melissa was willing to help, and we had to accept it. James left, assuring us he would text us to let us know everything was ok.

~ CALVIN ~

THE NEXT WEEK passed with me asking every fucking day when I could go home. I was never going to get the rest I needed and wanted at the hospital. I wanted out of there so I could get back to my life, *our* life. We still hadn't had a serious conversation about everything that had happened. I didn't want to push her, but when she sensed that I was going to, she would change the subject.

Jane walked in that morning, at the end of her shift, as I was staring out the window. I kept my stance as she wrapped her arms around me, leaning against my back. "I have a surprise for you!"

"It better be discharge papers." I turned so that we were face to face.

She moped before saying, "You're no fun. But yes, they're letting you go home!"

I wrapped my arms around her, "Thank God. Get me out of here."

"On one condition." I looked to her with the question in my eyes. "They're releasing you early. You have to take it easy and rest. Let me take care of you."

"Deal."

We were kissing gently when Jessica knocked on the door. "Sorry to interrupt, but I have your discharge papers."

LATER THAT DAY I woke from a nap and made my way downstairs. Jane was in the kitchen and it looked like she was cooking enough food for an army.

"What are you doing?"

She smiled as she scooped some food into storage containers. "Making you food. I want to make sure you have something to eat when I'm at work or sleeping."

I stood behind her and snaked my arms around her waist. "I can think of something else I want to eat." I nibbled on her neck as she tried to appear unaffected.

"Cal..." She was rendered speechless as I sucked and nipped on her neck and shoulder as my hands ran over her belly. "Cal, please. We have to take it slow."

Groaning, I rested my chin on her shoulder and watched her work. She brought the spoon to my lips as I indulged in the sauce. "That's really good. Thank you for all this."

"You're welcome. The fridge and freezer are stocked. I put reheating directions on them too."

"Easy peasy." I sighed, the fatigue was a horrendous burden that I was eager to be rid of.

"Go sit down."

I made my way around the counter to sit on the bar stool. "Don't you work tonight?" She nodded. "Ok."

"I'm off tomorrow and I invited some friends over."

She looked to me as I replied, "Its fine. It'll be good to see everyone. You should be sleeping if you're working tonight."

"I know. Once I'm done here I plan to lay down for a few."

I woke to her kissing me. "Hey, I have to go. If you need anything just call me." I didn't want her to go, but I knew she had to work. "Paul texted you. I told him you'd be home alone tonight. He's planning to come over in a while to keep you company."

"You're too good to me."

"Just behave and *relax*."

She turned and I grabbed her hand. "I love you, baby doll."

"I love you, too."

THE NEXT AFTERNOON Jane was sleeping and I was getting drowsy myself. The whole gang was coming over later that night and we needed our rest. I made my way to the bedroom and crawled into bed next to her. I pulled her close and immediately fell asleep with my arm around her.

I woke to her thrashing in the bed and when my eyes focused on her face, she was crying. I cradled her to me, whispering in her ear. She battled against me and when she woke, it took her several seconds before she realized it was me.

"Hey, you're safe." She relaxed, but moved to her side of the bed and turned her back to me. "Jane?" She didn't move a muscle. "Jane, I don't want to be a downer, but we've avoided it long enough." She turned her head and looked at me. "What happened with Derek?" I had a pretty good feeling what happened, but it needed to be out in the open.

She tilted her head before she said, "You know what happened, James came and..."

"That's not what I mean and you know it." She shifted uncomfortably before dropping her gaze to her lap.

"Baby doll, please. You can trust me." I moved so that I was leaning back against the headboard.

"I don't know what you're asking. Why I left him or w-what happened before you c-came to the house that night?" Her voice was beginning to tremble, which was so unlike her.

"Did he rape you?" She flinched at my words, or maybe it was my tone, and I knew that I didn't want to know, but I had to know for certain.

She glanced to me quickly and I saw her eyes filled with tears and it was the only answer I needed. She was raped because I went against my better judgment and didn't go after her quick enough. If I had followed her right after I realized she had left, it wouldn't have happened.

"God, I'm so sorry. This is my fault."

"It's not your fault. I should've told you sooner why I left him. If I'd told you…I should've told you." Her chin was quivering as a tear slid down her cheek.

My brain started reeling as it dawned on me that the abuse must have been a regular thing in their relationship. I dropped my head back as I gripped the sheets in my hands. Anger was burning through me at a rate I needed to slow down before I lost my cool.

"I'm sorry. I just wanted to move on and forget that part of my life. When you proposed, I freaked out. I couldn't say yes to you with those secrets between us. I-."

"Jane, please don't apologize. We can't change the past. Here and now is what's most important. I don't know what I was thinking proposing so soon." Her head shot up at that.

"Ask me again." Her words were barely a whisper. "I've been so shut off. I tried not falling for you, but you made it impossible." She was on her knees now, in front of me, both of us still on the bed. "I know I only said it a few times, but I love you. I do, Calvin. You saved me when I didn't think I needed saving. Please, ask me again."

She was swiping at tears as she dropped her eyes to my chest. I lifted her chin so that her eyes looked into mine. "I know you do. Say it again."

She smirked and whispered, "I love you, Calvin David Charles."

I pulled her close, so that she was sitting on my lap, before kissing her. "I love you too, baby doll." I wiped her tears away and wrapped my arms around her, trying to ignore the pain in my chest.

"P-please ask me again. I'll never forgive myself if I ruined my chance with you."

She was sobbing in my ear, clinging to my neck, and my heart broke for her. I didn't have any intention of letting her go, but she didn't know that. She was mine and would be mine in every sense of the word, but she wasn't ready. Not yet.

"Shh, Jane. I'm not going anywhere. You're stuck with me."

"Ask me again, I'll say yes." She pulled back and began searching my eyes.

"Jane. I'll ask you again, I promise, but not now. You're not ready." She needed to heal mentally and emotionally first. I *would* ask her again when I was confident that her and her secrets were no longer hiding away.

I got up and turned some music on, knowing that it helped relax her. *Dust to Dust* by The Civil Wars began playing. I had heard her listening to them a lot and hoped it helped calm her. Getting back on the bed, I pulled her close again. "Come here."

"I'm ready. I'm ready for you." She was choking on her own words as she clung to me.

"Jane, you're mine. Nothing is going to change that." She looked to me, searching my eyes. "Nothing."

Like the song said, we'd both been lonely a little too long. She'd already burned down my walls and captured every part of me. It was up to me to burn down hers and then I'd make her mine in every sense of the word.

~ JANE ~

CASSIDY AND I were in the kitchen preparing appetizers and snacks for the guests. Cal was upstairs napping and if he didn't wake soon, I was planning to go get him. Everyone had been invited. Frank, Paul, whom I had yet to meet in person, Jessica, some guys from SWAT, James and Cassidy and Cassidy's friends Lena and Anthony. Cassidy seemed a little on edge and I wanted to ask how things were with her and James, but decided against it.

"Cassidy, where's James?" Cal surprised us both with his sudden appearance.

She seemed unsure of what to say so I replied for her, "He's running a little late, but I have him picking up ice. He'll be here later." I wasn't sure if Cassidy became relieved or more anxious at my response.

It was still just the three of us when the doorbell rang. Cassidy was in the kitchen and I got up to answer the door.

"Jessica! You came."

"Couldn't pass up the free food." We laughed at that and before I knew it the doorbell was ringing again.

"You must be Jane."

"That's me. Pleasure to meet you, finally. Cal mentioned you were back in town. Sorry our paths never crossed at the hospital."

"No problem. I heard that crazy motherfucker got discharged for lewd and obscene acts."

I couldn't control the laugh that escaped my lips. I liked him immediately and knew why he and Cal got along so well. Paul closed the door behind him as Cal walked over. They traded handshakes and a hug, but Paul's eyes were looking for someone. His eyes stopped moving and his smile overtook his face. I turned and saw that he was staring at Cassidy.

Did they have a history? And if they did, why Cal hadn't told me was beyond me? Things would get messy when James showed. I watched Cassidy, who seemed frozen in place. They definitely had a history. God help them all. I knew how possessive and protective James could be. He'd lose his shit. I tried to ignore it and joined in on the conversation with Cal and Paul.

"Whenever you're ready to hit the weights again, I'm in."

"Definitely soon."

"Whoa. The doctors told you to take it easy, Cal."

"And I will, but I'm getting back to it on Monday. Monday work for you, Paul?"

"Yup."

"Men." I was annoyed, but knew I wouldn't be able to keep him down for long. I had to have faith that he wouldn't overdo it and listen to his body.

Paul walked away from us as Cal pulled me to the couch, but I couldn't take my eyes off the scene that played out in front of me.

"Cassidy Charles! Look at you."

She was beaming and flushed when she said, "Paul Vincent."

He hugged her while lifting her feet off the ground, swinging her around like they were kids. When her feet touched the floor, she didn't let go. Every mental warning was blaring in my head. He was a man on a mission and Cassidy was his endgame. Did he know she was taken?

"Jane?"

I turned back to Cal and Jessica, "What? Sorry. What was the question?"

four

~ CALVIN ~

I WATCHED, OUT OF THE CORNER of my eye, as Paul hugged my sister a little too long. Cassidy excused herself and ran up the stairs. Paul joined us in the living room and I gave him my stink eye, which he returned with that shit-eating grin of his. He'd find out soon enough she wasn't available. Speaking of, where the hell was James?

Cassidy was upstairs for too long so I went in search for her. I knocked on the bathroom door and asked, "Cass, you ok."

"Yup, I'll be out it a second." She sounded ok so I started to head back down the hall when I heard the door open. "Hey."

I walked back toward her as she tossed her arms in the air and whispered, "WHAT THE FUCK?" Her face exaggerating the words.

Whispering back I replied, "What?" Rolling her eyes, she grabbed my arm and pulled me into the bathroom with her.

"You're lucky I'm not smacking you right now. How long has Paul been in town and why didn't you warn me?"

"Warn you? You and Paul are ancient history. You're with James." She didn't have anything to say to that. "He's here on business. Cool your jets. I didn't think you'd care."

"Well, a little heads up next time might be nice. A girl needs a minute—or a hundred—to prepare for seeing the guy she lost her virginity to."

My stomach flipped as I gave her a dirty look, saying, "Dammit Cass, I don't want to know that." I stuck my fingers in my ears as the gravity of her words hit me and I dropped them. "That fucker. I *knew* it. I'll kill him."

Laughing, Cassidy said, "Really? Like you didn't know. It's ancient history. Remember?"

Snarling, I grabbed her hand and pulled her out of the bathroom. "Come on. I'm starving."

An hour or so later, I was chatting with Frank and Paul when Jane walked over to Cassidy and her posse—my friendly description of the trio she formed with Lena and Anthony. Frank had to run and left, then. The four of them were eating Paul and I alive, clearly they were up to no good and I wasn't about to let them pull Jane into their debauchery.

Remaining on my side of the room I bellowed, "What are you four up to? I knew those three too well and nothing good came from them conspiring together. Don't let them pull you in Jane." I walked over to her and wrapped my arm around her.

"We were discussing piercings." Cassidy elbowed Anthony and gave him a dirty look as I nearly swallowed my tongue. "What, where, gauge size and on whom." Anthony pointed his finger at Paul and me and then Paul walked over to join us.

"What about piercings and gauges?" Paul was incorrigible.

"Oh, my God. Knock it off you guys." Cassidy was embarrassed and blushing to boot.

"Cassidy, just ask and you shall receive." I rolled my eyes as Paul egged them on.

"I didn't ask. It was these two troublemakers." Cassidy pointed at Lena and Anthony.

"If I ask, will I receive too?"

"Well that depends on if you'll keep my secrets."

"Don't egg him on, Paul. You'll regret it." I couldn't help but laugh as I pulled Jane to the couch.

"Cal, do they have a history?"

I just shrugged my shoulders in response to her question then asked, "Where's your cousin anyways?"

"I don't know. He said he was coming."

"Well, you're my focus. They can figure out their own issues. Come here." I pulled her close and buried my head in her hair.

I must have started dozing off because before I knew it Jane was dragging me up the stairs to bed. Checking my watch I saw that it was close to midnight. She closed the bedroom door behind her as I sat on the bed.

"So, that wasn't awkward or anything."

"Tell me about it." I gave her a cliffs notes version of what had happened between Cass and Paul, which I still didn't fully know.

She walked over and helped me pull the shirt over my head. I was beginning to crave her like never before. I needed to feel her, all of her. Circling my arms around her hips I laid my head on her stomach and pulled her close. She momentarily resisted before I felt her fingers running over my scalp. My hands ran down her hips and legs and back up the back of her thighs as I squeezed her ass.

"Please be patient, Cal."

I knew I couldn't rush her and just thinking about why I couldn't was driving me mad. I wanted that fucker in the ground.

"I will. I'm not going anywhere."

THE NEXT EVENING, before her scheduled shift, I heard the water running and climbed off the couch. Jane was in the bathroom running a bath. She was wearing one of my t-shirts that hung to mid-thigh. She'd spent the early part of the day at the hospital. Her Aunt Eva—James' mom—had been admitted to the hospital the previous night, which was why he never made it to the party. She turned around just before I walked out of the bathroom.

"Get back here." I knew that smile. She had something up her sleeve. "I owe you a sponge bath." She perched her hands on her hips as I processed her words.

"Yes, yes you do." She walked over and helped me undress. If she wasn't intending to be seductive she was failing miserably because I was seduced.

Narrowing her eyes at me when she saw the state I was in, she said, "No chance, not happening. Doctors told you to take it easy."

"I plan on taking it easy. That's why you're going to do all the work." Shaking her head as she laughed, she gathered up some towels and washcloths before ordering me into the tub.

I eased down in as the water came up to my navel, just below the scar that ran the length of my chest. "Be careful, we want to keep it dry." She got on her knees on the side of the tub and got a rag wet. "Lean forward." I did as she asked as she carefully ran the rag over my shoulders.

She began rubbing my shoulders and back while I pulled my knees up to rest my head on them. I could feel myself dozing off as she began washing my legs.

"Don't go to sleep. I'll never be able to carry you to bed." I grunted. "Calvin, wake up or you'll leave me no choice." That peaked my curiosity, a little, but I was wiped out.

"God dammit, woman!" I flung the ice cold rag off my face; sleep now the last thing on my mind. She was snickering, still knelt down by the tub.

"Come on. Let's get you in bed."

As she stood up, I wrapped my hand around her wrist and waited for her to look at me. Her eyes got big and I pulled her in the tub before she could escape my grasp. "That's better."

"Calvin!" She was looking to my now soaked chest, but my healing incision was the furthest thing from my mind.

"I'll be fine." I cupped her face to mine and demolished her lips. The moan that she released was primal. "I've missed you, baby doll."

In a breathy voice, she whispered, "Cal, oh…"

She maneuvered herself so that she straddled my lap and wrapped her legs around my waist. I glided my hands to her thighs, ignoring the discomfort in my chest, and moved up to her hips, tearing the panties from her body without hesitation. She lifted up and I threw the shredded fabric to the floor. I tugged my shirt she wore over her head and buried my face in her breasts, listening to her heart ram against her chest. When I pulled back to kiss her again, tears were falling down her cheeks.

"Baby?"

"I never thought I'd get to hold you again, kiss you again, love you again, and have you inside me again." She placed kisses on my face before giving me the slowest and most sensual kiss of my life.

The bath water had become chilly and a shiver ran over both of us. I reached my hand out behind her and turned the shower head on. We both jumped when the ice water hit us, but quickly, it turned warm.

Pushing the hair out of her face, I left my hands on either side of her jaw as my tongue lapped the dripping water off her neck. I worked my lips up till I found her mouth again.

The walls that she had up, just the day before, seemed to be gone. She reached between our bodies and guided my cock to its salvation. Slowly, I pushed into her as I watched her eyes. It had been too long and she felt better than I remembered. Once I filled her, completely, we sat still and reveled in the feeling of our joined bodies.

Sitting back against the wall of the tub, I observed the water rain down on her. I watched the droplets of water as they rolled down her shoulders, over her breasts, and down to her belly. Slowly, she began riding me and quickly drove herself to the brink. She was my one and only weakness and my one and only strength.

"I love you, Jane"

Grabbing my face, she locked her eyes with mine. As she clenched around me, her eyes rolled back and she threw her head back, crying out my name. My release snuck up on me, and took me then, as her body fell to mine.

"I love you, Calvin."

~ JANE ~

WE SAT, CLINGING to each other, until the pads of our fingers became wrinkled. "I love you, Jane. Nothing will ever change that. You're mine to cherish and protect. I'm sorry I failed you that day."

Grabbing his face, "You didn't fail me. I should've trusted you with my secrets. I'm sorry." The guilt was written all over his face as I kissed his closed eyes. He wasn't the only one feeling guilty. It had been eating me alive, the things Derek did to me, the things I couldn't stop him from doing.

Being one with Cal was the only thing that seemed to make it go away, if even for just a few minutes. We climbed out of the tub, wrapping towels around our bodies, before walking to the bedroom.

"Jane, are you ok? I didn't hurt you did I?" His words surprised me as I stood by the dresser pulling out clothes for him and scrubs for me. He sat on the edge of the bed, just staring at me. "I mean, after what he did to you, I…"

I closed the distance between us and dropped to my knees in front of him, meeting his eyes. "Cal, physically I'm fine. You didn't hurt me. I promise. And just so you know, they tested Derek and myself at the hospital. Everything, so far, has been negative. But we really should stop being so careless." His eyes searched mine. "We haven't even discussed having kids or not. We should make that choice together, before it's made for us."

"I know, you're right. I'll pick up some more condoms."

"I can go on the pill too. It's no big deal."

"If you're comfortable with that, so am I."

Nodding, I wrapped my arms around him. "Today, in the tub, was the first time in weeks that I've felt like myself. Being one with you."

"I don't know what I'd do without you, baby doll."

Pulling away, I stood in front of him and whispered, "Let's not find out." I took his hand and yanked him to his feet. "Do you have the energy to dance with me?"

A soft smile spread over his lips. "Always. Do I get to pick?"

Nodding, I replied, "Your music is growing on me."

Laughing, he bellowed, "*MY* music. Well, that's a good thing." I watched as he fiddled with his iPod, picking a song. He walked back over saying, "*Come a Little Closer.*"

I obliged as he pulled me against him, both of us still in our towels. I let myself fade into him and the lyrics of the song and I soon realized that 'Come a Little Closer' was the title of the song. He was singing the lyrics, as well, and I couldn't remember a time I'd been happier. Things were back the way they were meant to be, at least that was my hope.

I hated doing it, but a couple songs later I pulled away. "I have to get ready for work." I kissed him and then we both got dressed.

He walked me to my car and stood on the porch waving as I pulled away. It had been bitterly cold that last week and I didn't want him out in the cold too long, but he had insisted.

IT WAS A pretty quiet night in the NICU. Only one mother was in labor and she was 36 weeks, so there were no concerns and the babies we currently had were all doing well. It just meant we'd get slammed with deliveries a few days later.

I was wandering the halls on my lunch break, remembering my evening with Cal. I had been so scared to open myself to him sexually again, but it was exactly what I needed.

There was something I had to do. Cautiously, I made my way to his room, which was on the same floor that Cal had been on. I was surprised to see that there was no guard. Derek was supposed to be under lock and key. I glanced into his room and he appeared to be asleep, but I could see he was cuffed to the bed. I made my way in, closed the door behind me, and approached his bed.

He had a small bandage remaining on his head. I looked at his chart and all his vitals had been normal, it probably wouldn't be long before they transferred him to county. I stood there, staring at the man I no longer recognized. What had happened? He was never violent with me, not until we moved to California. It didn't matter anymore.

He was going to spend a long time in prison, if I had anything to say about.

My stomach churned, but my heart was empty for him. I had nothing to say to him. It wasn't worth my energy. Placing his chart back on the end of his bed, I turned to leave.

"You came." The sound of his voice made my skin crawl.

Without turning, I responded, "It was a mistake."

I heard him laugh as he said, "The only mistake made was not killing that cop of yours."

So much anger rose up in me that it scared me. Turning to face him, I made my way to his bedside and spit out, "After everything you've gone through, you're still filled with hate. You almost died, almost killed me, and nearly killed Cal. And for WHAT? What did I do to you that was so horrible, that you felt the need to harm me and Cal?"

"Whenever you lay with him you'll remember I was there first."

"You're pathetic."

"You're mine, Jane. Always will be."

"That's where you're wrong. I'm MINE, not yours and not his. I choose who I give myself to, and it's not YOU. Not anymore and never will be."

"Once a skank, always a skank."

I saw red and leaned over him, knowing I was getting too close. "But not *your* skank."

I went to stand back up and saw his eyes get big with rage. His free hand grabbed the back of my head, gripping it tightly trying to bring me closer. Resisting with everything I had, I spotted the bedside phone and reached for it, but it was too far away.

"I'm going to put you both in the ground if it's the last thing I do. And you're going to watch as I end his life, or maybe he'll watch me end yours first."

I saw the call button—that also served as the TV remote—dangling above his pillow. I let him pull me closer so that I could reach it. Once my fingers clasped it, I smashed it against his head. Instinct had him loosening his hold on me and I pulled away.

"You fucking bitch."

"It's a pity James didn't kill you, but I'll get more pleasure knowing you'll be raped everyday like you raped me. I'm guessing they won't show you the same courtesy you showed me."

The door swung open then and I turned to see Jessica walk in. She must have been his night nurse. When she saw me, she closed the door and walked over.

"Jane, you shouldn't be here."

"She came in here and attacked me with no cause."

Jessica gave him the most disgusted look. "You're lucky I'm not attacking you, pig." She pulled me toward the door and looked me over. "Are you okay? You're bleeding."

She lifted my arm as I saw a few scratches on my forearm. "I'm ok."

"Jane, cover this up and pull your sleeves back down. I'll try to cover for you, but you could get in serious trouble if anyone finds out you were in here."

Nodding, I pulled my sleeve down as she looked into the hall for the all clear. "Thank you. I'm sorry. I was getting ready to leave when he woke up."

"You don't have to explain it to me. Get back to work. This never happened. You were never here."

~ CALVIN ~

I COULDN'T SLEEP that night. Tossing and turning my thoughts were with Jane and the things she'd told me. Derek had raped her, tortured her in the worst way possible. I already knew what had happened, but the gravity of it was just then hitting me. I didn't know if it was because she finally told me or if my senses were back enough to digest it all.

Getting dressed, I marched downstairs and called Paul. He was the only one I could trust. He answered, even though it was the middle of the night.

"Can you come get me? I have something I need to take care of."

When he arrived, I hopped in his SUV and he asked, "What's going on?"

"Can I trust you to have my back?"

"Of course man."

"I need to go have a *chat* with Derek."

"Calvin."

"Paul. He raped her, more than once. And I'm guessing the abuse wasn't new to her."

"What are you going to do?"

"I don't know, but I need your help."

He ran his hands over his face before letting out a big breath. "Ok. Let's go."

Chapter Five
~ CALVIN ~

A S WE GOT CLOSER TO THE HOSPITAL, murder was running hot through my veins. I wanted him dead. The music probably wasn't helping any. *Fire it Up* by Black Label Society was blaring through Paul's speakers. The cop in me knew it was wrong, but the boyfriend and lover in me didn't give a shit. The hospital was pretty vacant, given the hour, and I prayed no one would bother us.

We made it to his floor and I recognized the guard standing outside his room. Paul and I walked over to him and he nodded.

"Cal, you know you shouldn't be here." We shook hands. "You're looking good, though."

"Thanks Brian. Can I just have five minutes?" He was younger than me, and a rookie. I had bonded with him over a year ago. "You married, have a girlfriend, or a sister?" He nodded. "I know you understand."

Brian was shifting uncomfortably. "Five minutes. Don't make me regret this."

"I appreciate it. I just want to talk to him."

"I'll be back."

Paul and I watched as he went for a walk. Paul stood outside Derek's door as I went in. To really get a good look at Derek sickened me. He was bigger than Jane and used it to intimidate her, though I was even bigger. Jane was something to be treasured and protected and he used and abused her.

Kicking his bed, Derek's eyes bolted open and focused on me. He tried to remain calm but I could smell the fear on him. I leaned in close and asked, "Remember me?"

Before I knew it, he was saying things to me, baiting me and it worked. Soon one hand was circling his neck as the other held down his free arm. His face changed from white to red and was turning purple as I felt arms pull me off him.

"Cal, let him go. He'll get what's coming to him."

I knew Paul was right and I released Derek's neck from my hold. He began coughing and gasping for air as Paul pulled me away. Brian came through the door then and began cursing me when he took in the scene.

"Dammit Cal. You trying to get me fired? Get out of here."

"Sorry. He's alive." Derek was still holding his throat, catching his breath as Paul and I exited the room.

We didn't see anyone as we left. I was so angry I didn't even hear Paul talking to me until he shouted my name.

"CALVIN!"

"WHAT?"

"Dude, you could've killed him."

"Eye for an eye." I squatted down, running my hands through my short hair. "FUCK."

"You need to hit something."

"That's an understatement."

"I can swing by tomorrow and we can head to the gym. Sound like a plan?"

"Yea. Come by around lunch. Jane will be sleeping."

He dropped me off back at my place and inquired, "You're not going to do anything stupid are you?"

"Ha. I already did that. I'm staying home. Thanks, man."

"Anytime."

I woke in the morning to someone banging on the front door. Jane was asleep next to me. I hadn't even remembered her getting home. My late night excursion had taken its toll on me. Who could be at the door? Maybe Paul was early. I threw on some sweats and a tank top and headed downstairs.

When I opened the door, Frank was there in his uniform. Cassidy was walking up the steps behind him and I spotted James in the driveway. What the hell was going on?

"Where's Jane?"

Why did Frank need to see Jane? "She worked last night. She's still sleeping."

Frank huffed out a disgruntled breath and my stomach churned. "I need you to sit down."

"Frank, what the fuck is going on?" A pain shot through my chest and I brought my hand up to rub it away.

"Cal?" Cassidy rushed to my side.

"I'm okay. Just some pain. I'll be fine." Turning my attention to Frank I ordered, "Out with it."

"Derek's dead. It's all over the station. I shouldn't even be here. I could get suspended."

Jesus Christ. He was alive when I left, I knew that. We all stood there speechless, just staring at Frank.

"He's dead?" Turning, I saw her standing on the stairs and walked over to her, leaving my spot on the couch.

"It's over, baby doll. He's never going to hurt you again." I pulled her close to find she was shaking like a leaf.

"I should go. I was already taken off the case and they were already throwing around the names of the suspects."

"Suspects?" Cassidy stared at him, confused.

"There was a struggle. Derek was murdered."

James was enraged and he wasn't alone. "After what that fucker did, it's not murder. It's justice."

"And that's what's going to get you arrested. I'm looking at the top three suspects." We all stood and looked from one to the other. "You better get your alibis and stories straight." With that, Frank left.

I watched Cassidy drop herself to the couch, but she wasn't my biggest concern. Jane was still trembling and I knew who Frank was insinuating as the suspects. James, Jane and myself.

"Jane, let me call Annie."

How could James think she needed an attorney? Jane wasn't capable of murder. "She doesn't need an attorney, she didn't do anything." Jane started mumbling, but I couldn't make it out. "Jane, what's wrong?"

I pushed her away just far enough to see her face as she whispered, "I went to visit him last night."

"What?"

"Why?"

"I don't know. I had some things to say to him and I said them." She glanced at her arm and I noticed a bandage there. "He got physical and, and, but. He was alive when I left."

That made two of us. Where had Brian been? "Where was the guard watching his room?"

"He wasn't there. I didn't think about it."

"God dammit." Did she say he got physical? I was pacing when I stopped and removed the bandage from her arm. There were scratches on her arm and if Derek put them there that meant he had Jane's DNA under his fingernails. I looked to James and he was on the same wavelength as me. I nodded and said, "You better call Annie."

"I didn't kill him. I promise." Jane was frightened and becoming erratic.

"I know, but if he scratched you, well, all fingers are going to be pointing at you." Jane started sobbing and I wrapped my arms around her. I then wished I had killed him so that I could protect her.

James pulled out his cell phone and stepped outside. I had to get Jane upstairs and calm again. We would sort it out. I hoped. I took her back to the bedroom and we sat on the bed. She began sobbing and professing that she hadn't killed him.

"I know you didn't." She was too distraught. I couldn't tell her that I went and saw Derek too because then she'd just worry for me. "Everything is going to be fine. You should try to get some rest. I'll be back up in a few minutes."

"Will you hold me, please? Just for a minute."

"Of course." It wasn't long at all before she was asleep.

As I was walking back downstairs there was another knock at the door. Opening it, I was relieved to see Paul standing there with his gym bag in hand. He was smiling from ear to ear, like he always did, until he spotted Cassidy and James. Well, it was about time he figured out she wasn't available.

"Sorry. I thought you could use a workout buddy. You said today, right?"

"Yea, come on in. You haven't met Cassidy's boyfriend yet."

"No, it's okay. I can come back." Did he already know she wasn't available?

Cassidy chimed in, "Paul, please come in." He glanced to James as Cass continued, "Cal, Paul and James actually served together too. Paul is working for James."

What the fuck? I looked between all of them and had the urge to crack up laughing and cringe at the irony of it all. "Oh. Well, alrighty then. Your timing has always been impeccable, Paul."

I patted Paul's shoulder as he replied, "Tell me about it."

"You should sit down. I have some news." Paul needed to know what was going on, considering what had happened the night before.

James barked, "This is a family matter, Cal."

"I trust Paul with my life. After what we've been through, I would think you do too."

Cassidy seemed a little confused before she said, "James, you can trust him."

"I'm sorry. We're all under a lot of stress. Of course, I know I can trust him." James walked over to Paul and put his hand out between the two of them. "I'm sorry, man. No hard feelings."

"Nah, it's cool." They shook hands and then Paul asked, "So, what the hell has you all so serious?"

Annie arrived a little while later and James and Cassidy left as Annie and I sat down to talk, with Paul nearby. I filled her in on what I knew and answered her questions.

"I paid Derek a visit last night." She let out a breath, looking between Paul and me before urging me to continue. "The guard on duty is a friend, Paul was with me too. Derek was alive when we left."

"Does Jane know?"

Shaking my head, "She's pretty upset. I don't want her worrying about me too. She's not capable of murder, Annie."

"Well, if you're confident that the guard on duty will corroborate your story, you should be fine. But Jane is another story." Jane came downstairs then and joined in the conversation. "I don't want any of you talking to the cops without me present. Do I make myself clear?"

We all agreed as there was another knock on the door. The detective had some questions for us and we answered them with Annie's guidance.

Later that night, before her scheduled shift, Jane got a phone call from her boss, Sylvia. I was listening to the conversation and knew it was bad. They fired her, or at least that's what it sounded like.

"Yes, I understand." She sniffed and was trying so hard to control her emotions. "Ok, thank you. Bye." She hung up the phone and just stared at it after placing it on the counter.

"Jane?"

She looked to me and tried to smile, but it proved difficult for her. "They're putting me on a leave of absence."

Thank God they hadn't fired her. I knew how much her job meant to her. "That's good. Better than the alternative." She nodded as I walked to her and pulled her close. "It's going to be ok. Promise."

~ JANE ~

I COULDN'T WRAP my brain around the thought of Derek being dead. After thinking he was dead, when James shot him, to then find out he wasn't, my brain was in denial. I woke to the fading image of him hovering over me and heard voices from downstairs. Shaking the nightmare away, I headed downstairs. Annie, Cal and Paul were sitting at the table talking.

Cal walked over and took my hand. Sitting back down in the chair, he pulled me to his lap as Annie asked me a few questions. Shortly after some detectives showed up and asked some questions, though I don't remember many of them.

"Detectives, my client is still recovering from a trauma and months of abuse at the hands of *your* victim. Unless you're pressing charges, we're done here."

CAL WAS REHEATING some dishes for dinner when my phone rang. It was the hospital and dread weighed down on me as I answered the phone. Sylvia was very understanding, but given the circumstances they had to put me on unpaid leave. It was either that or I was going to be terminated. I didn't need the money, but I loved my job. I prayed that soon everything would be clear and I'd be able to go back to work. I set the phone down, trying to digest everything Sylvia had said.

"Jane?"

I tried putting my brave face on, which was almost impossible for me to do anymore around him. "They're putting me on a leave of absence."

He seemed relieved. "That's good. Better than the alternative." I nodded as he came to me and wrapped his arms around me. "It's going to be ok. Promise." It had to be. I hadn't gotten Cal back just to lose him again.

I stood there, leaning into him with my eyes closed. I never wanted to run away so bad in my life, but this time I wanted to take him with me. Lord knew I had the money and resources if I wanted it. We could buy one way tickets to anywhere and never come back. A girl could dream.

"So. We never exchanged Christmas presents. There were a few under the tree before, well. Now everything's gone."

How could I have forgotten Christmas? Mom had helped me take the tree down when Cal was still in the hospital and we'd boxed up the gifts and put them in the spare room. "I suck."

"You don't suck. It's been a crazy couple weeks."

"You can say that again." I pecked him on the lips and said, "I'll be right back."

Dragging the bag behind me, I pulled it down the stairs and sat down on the couch next to him. "Whatcha got there kid?"

Laughing, "Like you don't know."

He helped me place all the presents on the coffee table. There weren't too many since I had given him most of his gifts at the family party. The only ones left to give him were the concert tickets, and, well I couldn't remember what else I'd gotten him.

"Good grief woman." He picked up the heavy box and it was then I remembered the boudoir photos I'd had done. "What's in here?"

Laughing, I responded, "Open it and find out." I became increasingly nervous, not remembering all the different poses I'd done. "Wait, open this one first." I found the other large box, that wasn't heavy and handed it to him.

He eyed it before tearing the paper off. "Is there even anything in here? It weighs nothing."

I just smiled and waited as he pulled the box open. Picking up the envelope sitting on the tissue paper, he opened it to find four concert tickets to Kip Moore inside.

"Wow. How'd you know I like his music?"

"I have my ways."

"This is great."

"I got four and figured we could bring Cassidy and James with us, or whoever you want." He kissed me before I said, "There's more in there."

Pulling back the tissue paper, he exposed the top of the cowboy hat I'd gotten for him. Taking it from the box, he looked it over before trying it on.

"I wasn't sure on the size, I hope it fits."

"It's perfect." He was beaming.

"I figured you'd need it for the concert."

"Well played, woman." I kissed him as he handed me a box. "Here."

I took the small box from him and wondered what it could be. I opened and saw a small velvet box inside. My heart began to race when I realized it couldn't be what I thought because he had the ring on him the day of the shooting. In fact, it dawned on me that I didn't know where the ring was. I shook the memory away and pulled out the small box and opened it. Inside were a pair of modest pearl and diamond earrings. They were beautiful.

"Cal…"

"I thought they'd go with the pearl necklace you always wear."

"They're beautiful. They'll match perfectly." I threw my arms around his neck. "I love them. Thank you."

Pulling my arms from his neck he mentioned that there was more in the box. Smiling at him, I dug through the box. In the bottom was a USB flash drive. I looked to him with my lips pursed and eyes narrowed.

"It's a mixed tape, so to say. It's full of some of my favorite songs. Ones that remind me of you, some that I want to make new memories of *with* you," he waggled his brows at me, "that sort of thing."

I laughed, "You beat me to the punch. I have a playlist on my iPod dedicated to you, too." I set it down on the table and teasingly said, "I hope it's not full of country music."

Grabbing my hips he said, "You said it was starting to grow on you."

I was giggling as I tried prying his hands off of me. "It is. I was kidding. I love it. I'll have to transfer it over to my iPod."

"Here." He grabbed the flash drive and plugged it into his entertainment system. "We can start listening now." He was grinning from ear to ear as music began to fill the air. "Alright. Hand me that big one. I want to know what's in there!"

I was twiddling with my hair as he pulled the album out and looked at me confused. Motioning him to open it, he did just that. His mouth popped open as he stared at the pictures. A moment later he flipped to the next page. I couldn't bear to look at what picture he was staring at.

"Holy shit." I buried my face in my hands. He hated them. "Jane… Are you trying to kill me?"

My head popped up and my eyes met his. "I'm sorry. I wanted to surprise you and thought you might like them."

He scoffed, "Might like them. They're badass. I'm speechless."

My eyes drifted to the page that was open. I had my back to the camera, my hair flowing down my back in nothing, but my red lace trimmed panties. My hands were cuffed behind my back as well.

I watched as he traced his index finger down the picture. He had mentioned wanting to use cuffs on me in the bedroom so I thought the picture would be a good idea. Of course, after everything that happened, I didn't know if I'd ever be ready to bring handcuffs into the bedroom.

"Baby doll…" I lifted my eyes to his as he leaned in closer. "I think I have a *New Favorite Memory*." Before I could ask what he meant, he pulled us to our feet and started the song that was playing over, "Dance with me."

I loved that side of him. He was a hopeless romantic whether he knew it or not. In that moment, I knew that I was the luckiest girl in the world. I still felt undeserving of his love, but Lord knew I wanted it, needed it, and I would cherish it.

A FEW SONGS LATER, HE PULLED AWAY slightly, and lowered his mouth to mine. His kiss was soft, yet possessive. My hands found their way under his shirt as I held him close to me. When my lips were swollen and thoroughly used, he took my hand and pulled me up the stairs. We took our time as we undressed each other. My eyes fell upon his scar and my fingers traced his skin gently. A permanent reminder that he was willing to die for me, almost died for me.

I wasn't aware that I was crying until he stole the tear from my cheek. "Don't cry, baby doll. I'm all better." I looked up to him as I wiped away another tear. "Because of you. I'll never let anything happen to you."

"Let's run away. I have the money. We can go anywhere and no one would ever find us."

He was smiling when he replied, "Jane. We can't run. You didn't kill him. They'll figure that out soon enough."

"But my DNA is under his finger nails. Your faith in the justice system is stronger than mine."

"Please, let's not do this. Everything is going to be fine." He pulled me close and whispered in my ear, "I promise we'll run if we have too, but not until then. I'd go anywhere with you." I squeezed him tighter as he said, "Now kiss me, woman."

Chuckling, I pulled away and raised my eyes as I tilted my head. His eyes scanned my face as I asked, "Where?"

"What do you mean, where?" I raised my eyebrows and scrunched my lips together. "Oh, well. I may need to sit down for that."

I sat in bed that night and watched him sleep, like I did so many other nights. The nightmares consuming me made it difficult for me to sleep. The love for him that filled me was overwhelming. Derek was gone and I didn't have to worry about him hurting either of us ever again. I tried not to think about the possible murder charge coming my way. Who was I kidding? I was scared to death and didn't know how to prove that I hadn't killed him, though I had every reason and motive to do so.

THE NEXT TWO weeks, we kept ourselves preoccupied with Cal's recovery and just being one. He was working out as often as he could, at home and at the gym, eager to get back to work. His scar was almost entirely healed, but he was still very tender. While he spent a lot of time with Paul, I spent a lot of time with Aunt Eva. She had hospice care at home and they were doing everything to make her comfortable, knowing her time would end soon. It was a travesty. She was a wonderful woman who did so much for the under-privileged kids in the area. She would be greatly missed by more than just myself.

With Cal's blessing, I had also begun to redecorate. I needed something to keep me busy besides visits with Aunt Eva and going to Zumba. All of his walls were a boring cream color. I was going to change that. I was also planning on replacing the furniture, but that would be a surprise for him. Better to ask for forgiveness than permission—as my Mom always said.

I was painting the bedroom when he got back from the gym that night. I could hear him and Paul in the kitchen chatting. The new furniture had been delivered while he was out. A couch, some end tables, and a bedroom suite. The bedroom furniture was pushed together in the middle of the room, the mattress in the hallway, while I finished painting.

"Just who I needed." They both looked up to me, each holding a bottle of water.

"I like the new couch." Paul was more observant than Cal, who looked to the living room, taking in the furniture for the first time.

"Thank you. There's more up here that I need help with."

"Jane. What did you do?"

Paul laughed as I headed back to the bedroom and shouted over my shoulder, "Come and find out."

"Maybe I should stay down here." I heard Paul say with a suggestive tone to his voice.

"Nope, this requires two men."

~ CALVIN ~

PAUL'S EYES GOT all big as we took in Jane's words. "Cool your jets." I punched him in the shoulder before I headed for the stairs. "At least that better not be what she means."

The smell of paint filled the air—odorless paint, my ass. I walked into the bedroom and noticed immediately that the furniture piled in the center of the room was all new. It looked like she was done painting as she was putting a lid on a can of paint. One wall was a bright turquoise and the others were in a lighter shade, complimenting it.

"Wow."

"Do you like it?"

How did I answer that? "It's bright!"

"Well, it's better than the boring cream walls!"

"No, you're right. It'll just take some getting used to." I pointed at all the furniture. "You've been bad."

"You can punish me later."

"Hey now. You said you needed help." Paul was teasing us as he took in the room.

"Right. You up to moving some furniture?"

The three of us set to moving the furniture about the room. It was a good thing the room was small and left Jane with few choices on where to place everything. Paul and I grabbed the painting supplies and headed downstairs.

Shouting after us, "Why don't you order something for dinner?"

"Anything in particular?"

"Surprise me. Paul, you're staying too."

I laughed and looked at Paul. "You heard her. You're staying. Got a hankering for anything?"

"Nah, I'm easy."

"Don't we know it?"

Smirking he retorted, "When you got it, you got it!"

THE NEXT NIGHT we were headed to Cassidy's place for a night in. James, Cassidy, Anthony, Lena, Delaney, and Smith were all there. We played a game I wasn't familiar with. It was called Cards Against Humanity. It was horribly funny, completely inappropriate and the most fun I could remember having in a long time. We'd already played two rounds, ate dinner, and everyone was drinking. I had even indulged in a beer, not being a big drinker.

Cassidy and James seemed to be in a good spot. It was just what we all needed to take our mind off of everything else that was going on. Everyone was teasing each other and having a good time when there was a knock at the front door. James seemed a little perturbed when he got up to answer the door. I didn't think anything of it until I heard those fateful words.

"We're looking for Jane Whitford."

I was immediately on high alert and watched as James attempted to block the door asking, "Can I ask what this is about?" They pushed their way past him as everyone looked upon the officers dumbfounded. "Jane Whitford."

She stood up from her sitting place next to me and I was right behind her as we walked toward the officers. I didn't recognize them and that made it even worse. My hand was on the small of her back and she was trembling, or maybe that was me.

"You're under arrest for the murder of Derek Hamilton."

"Whoa, whoa." They had it all wrong. I had to stop it.

James was beside himself. "This is insane. Jane didn't murder that bastard."

They had her turned around and were cuffing her. I tried reasoning with them, "Is this necessary? She's not going to put up a fight."

James muttered something to Smith about calling Annie and he went outside with Delaney right behind him. I would confess to his murder before I'd let Jane take the blame. She couldn't do hard time. Not that I would have an easy time with it either, being a cop and all.

"Jane didn't do it. I did it. I killed Derek." I didn't know what to make of James and his sudden confession. If it was true I couldn't blame him, but if it wasn't then he was a better man than I gave him credit for.

"James!" Cassidy and Jane both cried out his name.

"Sir, we have evidence on the contrary."

Jane went to protest and I told her to keep her mouth shut. "You should do the same, James. Wait for Annie."

He was a stubborn ass and kept talking. "Jane and Derek had an altercation. I walked in and stopped it, but not before he scratched her arm. I told Jane to go back to work and then I finished him off. I smothered him with a pillow, after knocking him out."

Cassidy hurled herself at him, fists beating his chest. "You liar. You're lying." James just stood there and took it from her. She was furious or putting on the best performance of her life. "Tell them the truth, right now."

"I am telling the truth. I'm sorry Cassidy."

Smith came back in and pulled Cassidy off of James as the officers discussed a few things in private. A moment later they walked back over and said, "If that's how you want to play this, that's fine. Jane Whitford and James Benedict, you're both under arrest for the murder of Derek Hamilton."

FUCK! They cuffed James and then Jane before walking them outside. I grabbed my keys off the counter knowing I'd follow them downtown and make some phone calls to see if I could get any more info.

I sat in my truck, waiting for them to leave. Annie answered right away and said she'd meet me at the station. Cassidy was standing on the porch and she looked like a shell of herself. She had no idea what was going on. My phone started ringing again and it was Paul.

"Paul, I can't talk right now. They just arrested Jane and James." He was as shocked as I was. "No, she's home. Dude, this isn't good. Yea, I'll stay in touch."

I got to the station, Cassidy refused to go with me. Everyone I talked to wouldn't spill any information. Stepping outside for some fresh air, I spotted Frank arguing with our supervisor. Frank got in his car and drove off before I could get to him.

"Charles. You know I can't tell you anything, but I hope she's got a good attorney. She's going to need it."

"She didn't do it!" He just waved his hands in the air before walking back inside.

Paul texted for an update and I asked him to check in on Cassidy. She wasn't returning my texts and I was getting worried. Annie walked in and just told me to sit down and shut up.

~ JANE ~

I COULDN'T BREATHE. Finally, we were all having a good time—which was needed by all—believing that everything would work out. James confessed to killing Derek and then they put the handcuffs on both of us. My heart was racing as the anxiety filled me at the memories of being confined.

"James?"

He wouldn't look at me, just warned me, "Jane, shut your mouth. Don't say a word without Annie. You understand."

"But..."

"Jane, do you understand?"

"Yes." The officers got in the car and pulled away with us in the back.

I was sitting in a holding cell for what felt like hours. They didn't talk to me, didn't question me, and just left me to my thoughts. I'm sure they were hoping I'd break, but I wouldn't confess to something I didn't do. Where was Annie? I needed to talk to Annie and Cal.

A little while later, I was taken into an interrogation room and Annie was waiting for me. She motioned me to sit down and didn't say anything until the door closed and we were left alone.

"I'm doing everything possible, but they can keep you for forty-eight hours." My eyes got big and she grabbed my hand. "Them doing this on a weekend is them playing hardball. Most judges won't stand to be bothered, not in this town. I'll do everything I can to get you out of here as soon as I can."

My voice wavered as I tried to speak. "W,what about James?"

"I can't tell you too much, but we have a plan and we're hoping it works. I'm waiting for the DA to get back to me. I need to know exactly what it is they have against you two."

"Ok." I tried to remain calm and asked her about Cal.

"He's not going anywhere. He's going to get himself arrested if he keeps harassing everyone. I'll try to keep him calm." I nodded as she said, "Try to stay calm. Don't talk to anyone and I'll be back in the morning."

I spent most of the night sitting on the bench, huddled in the corner. Grateful to be alone in my cell, but the silence was driving me insane. I got word the next morning that James had been released. I was happy for him, but Annie told me I'd probably have to stay another night. Annie was the only one they allowed me to see, though my mom, dad, and Cal had all tried numerous times to see me.

"They're convinced you're going to snap." Annie looked to me, trying to encourage me with her smile. I knew that she was referring to the cops. "They all send their love. I don't think they have enough evidence to press charges, so they're going to hold you as long as they can. If they had substantial proof they would've pressed charges by now. Let's hope that it plays in your favor that the hospital security footage has been tampered with."

"What do you mean?"

"Smith has a few friends here—that's not widely known so don't say anything—and the footage from the hospital is inconclusive. He's working on it, trying to find the real suspect. I sent Cal and Paul down the street to get dinner. He hasn't left yet, he stayed here all night."

That made me smile. "Yes, he's very loyal."

"It must run in the blood." She giggled at the expression on my face, knowing I was curious what she meant. "Cassidy marched in here this morning giving James an alibi. She perjured herself without thought."

"Oh God. What's going to happen to her?"

"Well, prepare yourself." I scrunched my eyes because she was suppressing a laugh. "Cassidy is now Cassidy Benedict."

"What?"

"I may have suggested that they get married so they wouldn't have to testify against each other."

We both stared at the other for a moment before we both started laughing. I couldn't believe James got married. I mean, if anyone was going to get him to settle down, I was grateful and knew, Cassidy would do it. But I was still shocked. They eloped with no question. That just seemed so extreme for both of them.

"Don't tell Cal. I'll tell him if Cassidy hasn't."

"Deal." Annie stood and opened the door. "Remember what I said. Be strong. I'll be back tomorrow."

I nodded as the guard came in to return me to my cell.

seven

~ CALVIN ~

Paul and I were sitting at the diner down the street. My appetite had taken charge once I realized I hadn't eaten in over a day. Paul was quiet, for the most part, and I was thankful that my friend was back in my life. During the chaos of the previous weeks, it had dawned on me, I hadn't asked him how things were going with him. He was working for James—that was an initial surprise—since they had been in the Army together too.

"So, how are things at work?"

Shrugging his shoulders, he finished his bite of food before talking. "Eh, it's work and I love what I do, but the whole James-Cassidy scenario threw me for a loop."

He eyed me curiously and I just nodded. I couldn't imagine how awkward things were when they put all the pieces together. Even I was surprised to find out that Paul knew James from their time in the service. I mean really, what were the odds?

"I don't think James trusts me, or maybe it's Cassidy he doesn't trust." I glared at him, knowing that my sister would never do anything to warrant James not trusting her. "He and I have a history, and now he knows about my history with Cassidy. It's a mess."

"Paul. She's spoken for."

"Give me a little credit, man. I won't encroach on his *territory*. Not without an invitation." I threw my napkin on the table, and when I looked at him, I knew he was goading me purposefully. "Anyways."

"Yeah, anyways." I didn't want to get tangled in the web that the three of them were weaving, but would if I had to. Paul wouldn't take what wasn't his. The question was did he *know* she wasn't his? Paul had been hurt before so he knew the anguish of it all first hand. The timeline started running through my head of what he went through with Cora. "Shit."

Paul looked to me and made the connection that I had put some pieces together. "Yes, he was there for all of it with Cora."

I couldn't help but ask, "He's not…"

Paul cut me off. "He wasn't the only one and he didn't know she was married. The others knew."

"Jesus. How did he not know?"

"I'm not one to defend him, but Cora really did a number on him, too. If he's untrusting, it's because of her, not your sister." He picked up his cup and took a long sip of his drink. "Listen. I've been needing to talk to you about that night at the hospital."

That got my attention and I asked, "What about it?"

"I went back up there after I took you home."

"Jesus Christ, Paul. Should I call Annie? Fuck, I don't think I want to know. Did *you* do this?" My blood was boiling at the thought of him letting Jane sit in jail, but he wasn't a murderer. Was he? He went to speak and I stopped him. "Don't, not another word until we call Annie."

THE NEXT MORNING, Annie was finally able to get Jane released. They weren't pressing charges, but she was still a person of interest. Before she was released, I had been questioned again. Brian, the cop working Derek's room that night, confirmed that I had paid Derek a visit. If I was planning to confess to killing him, I'd have to come up with another plan. Brian was suspended for a week and I was ridiculed by my sergeant.

Jane walked out and jumped in my arms. She clung tightly to my neck as I lifted her off the ground.

"Thank God, baby doll." I buried my head in her neck, thankful she was back in my arms. "Let's get you home. You smell like a jail cell."

That elicited a small giggle from her as I sat her back on her feet. We were walking to the parking lot with Annie, when a woman approached us. I felt Jane tense as the woman came closer.

"You won't get away with this!"

I tried to step between the two of them, but Jane stopped me. "Diane, I didn't do this. I promise you. I didn't kill your son."

"Jane, you don't have to speak to her." Annie was trying to diffuse the situation, as Derek's mother kept talking.

"You ruined his life. If you didn't kill him, I'm sure you know who did." She persecuted me with her eyes before turning back to Jane. "You're a little hussy, always were."

I was getting pissed. "Excuse me, Diane is it?" She lifted her chin and nodded. "Whatever you may think of Jane is fine, but *your son* was a monster. Are you aware of what he did to her, and what he did to me, in his madness?"

She didn't say anything for a moment and we started to walk away. "Lies. They're all lies. My Derek would never hurt anyone."

I turned on her and lifted my shirt, exposing my scar. "Nothing? You call this nothing?" Her eyes landed on the scar that donned my chest and abdomen. "And what about the scars he gave Jane? She turned and headed toward the station.

We began walking to my truck as her voice filled the parking lot once again. "You deserve each other. Now that I know who you really are, Jane Whitford, I'm glad that you aborted that baby. And if you hadn't, I would have fought you for the rest of my life for custody of that child. You're unfit."

I was speechless. Did Jane abort a baby? I followed her image as she disappeared inside. I was vaguely aware of Annie's voice consoling Jane. When my eyes found them, Jane was white as a ghost, tears streaming down her face.

"Jane." I didn't know what to say.

"Jane, she's grieving the loss of her son and clearly in denial about the monster he was. Don't listen to her." Annie was holding Jane's hand and then turned to me, "Cal, you need to get her home."

Nodding, we flanked Jane and walked her to my truck and I closed the door, once she climbed in. Annie was parked a few cars down and I stood watching her walk away. She stopped and walked back over to me.

"I don't need to know your personal business, but Jane's wounds, from Derek, go deep. Don't believe anything his mother said. There's more to the story. Always is. But, you need to be patient with her and she needs to trust you with her secrets or she'll never heal." I nodded and felt my own eyes filling with tears. Annie put her hand on my arm, "Losing a child, no matter the cause, can be devastating to a woman. I would know. If there *was* a child."

She walked away and got in her car as emotions I'd rarely felt, surged through me. Jane had never mentioned a baby to me. The only time we'd even discussed kids was when it came to preventing the conception of them. I didn't even know if she wanted kids. She worked with newborns, but that wasn't a guarantee that she wanted them. I scrubbed my hands over my face and took a deep breath before I climbed in the truck.

She was resting her head against the seat and staring off into space. I put my hand on her leg and squeezed gently. She put a hand on top of mine, but didn't make eye contact with me. I started the truck and drove us home. It was foreign territory for me and I didn't know what to do, but I knew I couldn't leave her alone and I had to get her to open up to me. When she was ready.

Jane was eerily quiet the rest of the day. She called her mom and dad and told them she was fine, but exhausted. I agreed that she wasn't up for company. I reheated some leftovers that she picked at before heading upstairs.

"I'm going to go take that shower."

She'd hardly made eye contact with me since we left the station. "Ok."

I watched her walk up the stairs and shortly after, the water turned on. I was totally unsure of what to do. How did I handle it? I didn't know how much space to give her. Was I giving her too much or not enough? She was always pretty guarded with her emotions and now she just seemed devoid of them.

The water was still running when I decided to go check on her. The bathroom door was ajar as I stepped through it. I saw her shadow through the almost translucent shower curtain and asked if she was ok. She didn't respond.

"Jane?" I heard the sounds of her ragged breathing and knew she was crying.

Without thought, I climbed in the shower with my clothes still on. The water was barely warm and I turned it up so that we wouldn't freeze. She was standing there, still clothed herself, and as I wrapped my arm around her, she slid to the floor. I slid down with her and held her close. The sobs that ripped through her were killing me. I didn't know what to do, how to help, to make it stop.

Pulling her closer I whispered, "It's ok, Jane. You're going to be ok. I've got you."

She attempted to speak and it came out scattered and erratic. "I did-didn't do the things she said. But, it's my fault. He's dead, you almost died, James. Me, it was all my fault. My fault."

"Baby doll, it's not your fault." She buried her face in my chest as I tried to soothe her.

We sat there for a while and I realized she was drifting off. I had to get her out of the shower, dried and warm before she got sick. The last few days and weeks had caught up to her. I knew she was exhausted. I managed to get to my feet and pulled her up as well. Throwing the curtain open I swooped her slight frame up into my arms and stepped out of the shower. I grabbed some towels and walked us to the bedroom.

Placing her on the bench at the end of the bed I wrapped a towel around her and removed my clothes before wrapping the other towel around myself. I turned some music on when I made it to the dresser because I knew how it soothed her. We'd both grown familiar with the playlists we each enjoyed and I found the one filled with slow and soothing tunes.

I pulled some pajama pants and a shirt out of one of her drawers and placed them on the bed. She didn't fight me as I removed the soaking clothes from her body. It was my turn to take care of her and I was grateful to do it.

Once I had her dressed, I pulled the covers down and put her in bed. "Get some rest. I'm going to lock up. I'll be right back."

She didn't acknowledge my words, but burrowed under the covers as her eyes began to struggle to remain open. I threw on some clothes, grabbed the wet clothes and towels, and took them to the laundry room. I made sure the blinds were closed, the doors locked, and shut everything off. It was early, but I didn't care.

When I got back to the bedroom, I turned the music down a little and saw *Turning* Page by Sleeping At Last come on. I climbed into bed, next to her, and wrapped myself around her back as I listened to the melodramatic tune. She let me pull her close and rested her head on my outstretched arm. My head was on the pillow just above hers as she searched out my other hand and tucked it to her chest.

"Get some rest, baby doll. I love you. You're safe with me."

When I woke several hours later, she was gone. Quietly, I stalked the rooms until I found her. She was standing in front of the living room window, gazing at the snow coming down. She appeared to be deep in thought. I watched as her hand traveled to her lower abdomen and rested there for longer than I thought was normal. She wiped at a spot under her eye and I wondered if she was crying. Maybe what Derek's mom had said was true or maybe what Annie said was true. No matter what happened in her past, it wasn't going to dictate our future.

~ JANE ~

THAT DAY WAS a fog after the confrontation with Diane in the parking lot at the police station. I remember climbing in the shower and realizing I hadn't undressed and not caring. The horrible things she said to me had sliced me wide open again. I didn't have an abortion, but she thought I had. I could only imagine the horrible things Derek had told her.

Cal, oh God, what had Cal heard? Did he believe her? He probably did and thought I was a horrible person. Maybe I *was* a horrible person. I'd caused so much misery to everyone around me. Maybe it would be best for everyone if they locked me up and threw away the key. That way I couldn't hurt anyone anymore, regardless that I was innocent.

I remembered him carrying me out of the shower and getting me dressed. It was humiliating, being so helpless. I couldn't get my body to move or do the things I wanted it to. Sleep, I just wanted to sleep. Soft music was playing and I focused my senses on that and the warmth of the bed. Soon, his warm body encompassed mine and I couldn't get close enough to him.

Nightmares from that horrible day over a month ago, invaded my sleep. I was standing over Cal as he bled out and Derek fired off another shot. I knew it wasn't real, but I couldn't stop the guilt that I felt over the whole situation. I woke up and saw that it was the middle of the night. Cal was still wrapped around me, but I managed to slip out of the bed.

I turned the music off and went to the bathroom. I walked through the townhouse and took in the place. Everything that had once been solely his was now ours. Little pieces of both our personalities decorated the entire place. Yet, he still didn't know everything about me. I felt like I was lying to him by omission. I wanted a child desperately and wanted it with him. But we needed time to enjoy *us* first. What if he didn't want kids?

My hand drifted to my belly. I remembered how I had just started to feel the physical changes in my body when I'd lost the baby at Derek's hands. The bump had been small, but I could feel it, especially when I laid in bed. A tear fell from my eye and I swept it away. I stood there for another moment when I thought I heard the wood floors creak. I turned, but didn't see Cal. Closing the blinds before making my way back upstairs, I found him in bed. I climbed in on my side, gently, not wanting to disturb him.

I kept my distance though I desperately wanted to feel him. Laying on my back, my eyes focused on the darkness that surrounded me. His hand drifted up my leg before finding my own. He wove his fingers through mine and gently pulled me to him.

"The past will fade away if you let it. I'm not going anywhere and if you need to talk, I'll listen."

My throat tightened at his heartfelt words. "I love you, Calvin. It's fading away. Slowly. Thanks to you."

eight

~ JANE ~

When I woke in the morning, I found Cal on his back, sound asleep. I propped myself up on my elbow and stared at him. Examining his tattoos, while my fingers trailed the outlines, he started to rouse. His scar seemed fitting as it ran down the middle of his chest and down his abdomen. He yawned and stretched his arms over his head as the muscles grew taut on his chest and abdomen. The sheet was lying across his hips in a seductive way. My fingers began trailing the V that his hips and muscles created. He was thinner than before, but more defined.

My eyes moved to his and I found him watching me. Removing the sheet, I found his morning erection straining against the fabric of his boxer briefs. I got on my knees and pulled them from his body as his cock bounced against him. Still wearing my pajama pants and shirt, I climbed on top of him so that I was straddling his hips.

He just stared at me as I molded my body to his. I adjusted my hips and wedged his cock between our bodies, just how I wanted. I wanted him, needed him. My hands gripped his hips as I wiggled against him, seeking a small amount of relief. My eyes closed at the sensation and I felt him throb against me as he took in a sharp breath.

"Jane."

His hands went to the waist of my sleep pants and fingered the exposed skin of my abdomen. His hands moved higher and delicately traced my ribcage. He rubbed a small circle over my lower belly and locked eyes with me.

"Jane, do you want kids?" My throat was dry and began throbbing as I tried to pull away from him. He stopped me from moving and said, "It's just a question, not an inquisition."

"I, it's just, I don't know? Do you?"

He smiled softly, "Only if you do. I'd have a dozen kids with you." I knew my eyes grew big and he laughed, "Or none. I just want you. If you want kids then I want kids."

His words weren't perfect, but they were what I needed to hear. Sniffling, I replied, "I want kids, very much. I'm not sure I want a dozen though."

We both laughed as he teased, "I don't know. That might be a deal breaker." He winked at me then, flashing those dimples and baby blues at me.

"Cal, on a serious note. What Diane said—it's not true."

"It's ok, baby. I don't care what she believes or says. I care about you, me, and us in the now. Forget her." I searched his eyes, debating if I should tell him about my miscarriage. It wouldn't change anything, only bring up pain I didn't want to discuss. "You going to kiss me or not."

Smiling, I looked to him, "Maybe I'm waiting for you to have your way with me!"

He laid there, motionless, then startled me when he gripped my hips and flung me to my back. I was pushing my hair out of my face as he came down over me. "Don't move."

He jumped off the bed and headed to the dresser. I watched as he lit some candles and hit play on the iPod. He was so sweet. The room was now illuminated by a few candles as soft music filled the room.

"Roll over." He pointed his finger at me motioning me to roll over. Smiling at him, I obliged and watched him pull some massage oil out of the night stand and placed it on top.

The bed dipped under his weight as he ran his hand under my shirt and grazed my lower back ever so lightly. His hands ran up and down my back before he pulled the shirt over my head. I heard him squirt some oil in his hands before he began rubbing my shoulders.

I moaned as he kneaded my muscles. He was good. "I think you've done this before, Officer Charles."

"I'll never tell."

He added more oil and worked his hands lower until he reached the waist of my pants. Just when I thought he would sink his hands into my pants, he moved them back up my sides, grazing the sides of my breasts. A ripple ran through me as I felt his hot breath at my ear.

"You're going to scream in delight before you feel my cock inside you, baby doll. I want you begging for it, knowing it's the only thing that'll satisfy you."

My body caught on fire at his words and became a heaping pile of desire. Brushing my hair aside, his lips found the back of my neck and he began sucking on me. I would be branded with his love bite when he was done. My hips moved against the bed and when he noticed the movement he cupped my ass and moved his hand toward the throbbing center of my body.

"So warm. Are you wet, too?"

I didn't dare answer him because I wanted him to find out for himself. He shifted his position and pulled my pants off my legs as I assisted him. He dripped oil over the backs of my thighs and began rubbing them. He was right. I was going to scream if I didn't have him inside me.

He continued rubbing my thighs and ass, getting closer and closer to my entrance with each stroke. I moaned into the pillow as his hand cupped me and pressed against me, sending a burst of ecstasy through me.

"Yup, definitely wet."

He rubbed my clit, long enough to have me nearly delirious, before turning me to my back. My hands gripped the headboard as I watched him gaze over my body. He grabbed the oil and poured it all over my front before his hands massaged it into my skin. Circling my breasts, my nipples were at high alert, waiting for his touch, and when his thumbs flicked over my nipples, I thought I was going to burst.

"Cal..."

"Not yet."

I groaned in protest as his hands moved down my abdomen to my hips. He began teasing my inner thighs with his oiled fingers. Lowering his head, his tongue licked the skin on my inner leg before he began sucking on my lower belly. I couldn't stop the convulsions that ran through me as his tongue moved closer and closer.

"Please, Cal. Please, I'm begging you."

He didn't say anything as his face moved up and closer to mine. His lips hovered over mine as his fingers began massaging my folds. I lifted my head, desperate to kiss him as his fingers slid inside me, but he denied me his lips. Instead, he just watched me fall apart under his touch. Plunging and twirling his fingers over and over again as I clenched around him. He added a third finger as his thumb circled my clit, causing me to still.

He ceased his movement asking, "Is it too much?"

Locking my eyes with his, as my body tensed around his fingers, I shook my head. "No, don't stop, Cal."

He began moving again and I gripped the headboard tighter. I threw my head back and rocked my hips against him as my body began to spiral out of control. His free hand came over my lower belly and pressed down gently as my body stiffened.

"Now. Cal, I'm begging now."

He didn't stop and as my orgasm flooded me, he never stopped touching me. My body felt weightless while my head felt like a lead ball. The waves surged through me for longer than I expected. I was vaguely aware of him sheathing himself and positioning himself between my legs. Lifting my hips, he sank into me as I cried out his name again.

"God, baby, how did I ever survive without you?" He pulled out and sank into me again as I gripped him tightly. "We were made for each other. Don't ever forget it."

My hands let go of the bed and found the back of his thighs as he plunged into me again. I couldn't get him close enough. "Don't hold back, Cal."

"I don't think I can hold on, baby."

The sweat dripped off his forehead as he pushed in and out of me. "Don't hold on. Fall apart." My hand traveled to my clit as I rubbed myself.

His eyes followed my hand, "Shit, Jane." I hesitated and he said, "Don't stop. I want you to come again."

He grabbed my hips and managed to pull me closer as I pleasured myself. I could feel myself reaching the end once again. His dick filling me up as I rubbed my clit, felt amazing. "Cal…"

"Do it." My eyes rolled back as my second orgasm took me. I felt the change in him as he growled out his release.

I was still circling myself as the final shockwaves twisted through me. His mouth found mine, the kiss was rough and tender all at the same time. I pulled my hand from between our bodies and he pulled his lips from mine. Grabbing my hand, he put my fingers in his mouth and sucked on them gently, causing me to moan.

"You're the devil."

Smirking as he released my fingers, "And you love it."

"Mmm."

I couldn't suppress the yawn that came next. He rolled to his back and took me with him, where we fell asleep twisted up in one another.

~ CALVIN ~

I WOKE AN hour or so later and crawled out of bed. She was still asleep and I observed her for a moment. She was the most important thing in my life. I wanted her to be my wife, have my babies, and cry out my name in the throes of ecstasy for the rest of our lives. The ring. Where was the ring? I had it with me that day, but I didn't have a clue what happened to it after. Maybe Dad or Cassidy knew where it was. If they didn't, I'd just have to get her a new one when the time was right.

Making my way downstairs, I checked my text messages. I had a text from James, and Smith, both. They had been working on the security footage of the hospital from the night of Derek's murder. It had been tampered with, the hard drive showing signs that it had a virus. We sent a couple texts back and forth and Smith confirmed that he would call me later for a conference call.

Deciding to call my dad, I updated him on the situation. He was grateful that Jane had been released. He voiced his concern for Cassidy and I agreed. She hadn't taken James confession very well.

"Dad, do you by chance know what happened to Jane's engagement ring?"

He chuckled, "Funny you should ask. Yes, I have it." Thank God. "The hospital gave it to me with your other belongings. I held on to it. Sorry. I should've told you that I had it."

"No, it's ok. I'm just glad it's safe." There was a moment of silence before I said, "I'm going to need it back."

"Alright. Just ease into it, Son. You've both been through a hell of a lot."

"Dad..."

"Don't get me wrong. I like Jane, a lot, and would be thrilled to have her as my daughter-in-law. Just enjoy getting to know one another."

"Um, there's no problem there."

"Ok, too much information." We both laughed. "Maybe Lisa and I can come down this weekend and we'll all have dinner."

"Sounds good."

Dad, Lisa, James and Cassidy all came over for dinner that weekend. In private, Dad gave me Jane's engagement ring back and I put it away in my dresser. We were all sitting around the table when James asked for everyone's attention.

"So, Cassidy and I have an announcement to make."

I looked to Cass and she seemed nervous, but was blushing. If he had knocked her up, he and I were going to have words. What could they possibly have to announce?

"You want to tell them?" She shook her head in response to his question. "Well, Cassidy is now Cassidy Benedict."

I dropped my fork and the clang rang through the air as everyone stared at them in disbelief. Everyone, but Jane. Did she know? Cassidy shrugged her shoulders as James pulled her close. I tried making eye contact with her, but she was avoiding my eyes. Something else was going on?

"I'm confused. You're married?" Finally someone asked the question we all wanted the answer to. Dad looked to them and narrowed his eyes at them, "Cassidy. What's going on?"

"It's like he said. We eloped on Sunday, after he was released."

Now I was even more suspicious. Maybe he really had killed Derek and Cassidy married him for what? As an alibi? I'd kill him for involving my sister.

"That was almost a week ago. Why are you just now telling us?"

"Well, we weren't going to tell anyone at first, but since you're all here. We told J.J. and Eva on Monday."

I'd heard enough. Standing, "Benedict, you, me, outside. Now."

"Cal." Jane and Cass were both trying to get me to sit back down.

"It's alright." James looked to me, "Let's do this. I expected nothing less."

I was a little surprised that Dad didn't join us, but I figured he'd have his own talk with James. We stepped onto the front porch and he closed the door behind him.

I stepped into his personal space and spit out, "I swear to God, if you've involved my sister in some murder cover up, I'll kill you."

He laughed and said, "Your sister did that, not me."

"What the hell are you talking about?"

He proceeded to explain how Cass went to the station and provided a false alibi for James. Worried they'd both end up in trouble, Annie had suggested that they get married so that neither of them could testify against the other. He told me how he had paid Derek a visit that night too, but swore Derek was alive when he left. It seemed to be the general consensus from everyone. What concerned me was my sister. I knew her and this wasn't some sham to her.

"I don't know what your plans are, but my sister better be your top priority. She's head over heels for you. This isn't temporary for her."

"I know it isn't. I don't need your advice on how to care for my wife."

Poking his chest with my finger, I growled out, "I'll remember you said that. If you screw this up your face will have an appointment with my fist."

"Cool your jets, Cal. He gets it." We both turned to see my Dad standing in the doorway. "James, can I talk to you."

"Of course."

I went back inside, leaving my Dad with James on the porch. Cassidy, Jane, and Lisa were laughing and giggling. Jane caught my eye and I knew in that moment that she had known. She mouthed 'sorry' and I took a deep breath and shrugged my shoulders. I knew she was stuck between a rock and a hard place. I had to have faith that my sister knew what she was doing. She wasn't a kid anymore, but more often than not she let her heart lead her, not her head. I guess you could say the same thing about me, considering I myself had proposed to my girlfriend of only six weeks.

OVER THE NEXT couple weeks we all tried remaining optimistic as Smith and his guys worked on the security footage. We had word that Melissa was diving in head first with Dan. She was determined to prove that he was behind Derek's murder. We were all uncomfortable with it, especially me. I knew firsthand how undercover operations could go wrong and that was with people who had training. Melissa didn't have any training and no one on the inside to protect her. But, she was also our best chance to get to Dan.

nine

Valentine's Day
~ JANE ~

OPENING THE LETTER, I WASN'T sure what to expect. The return address was from the property manager from my apartment in San Francisco. I'd received a letter about a month ago. Derek was behind on the utilities—convenient considering I'd paid through September— and they had interested buyers. I had purchased the apartment, but clearly had no use for it now. I had contacted them and made the arrangements to put it up for sale. Now I had to get my stuff out and Derek's too.

I would have to make arrangements to go soon. I wasn't officially on the schedule for work yet and wouldn't be until I wasn't a suspect anymore. I took a mental note to check with my supervisor anyway to see when would be the best time to go. There would be papers to sign and it would be the opportunity I needed to get the rest of my stuff.

Taking the letter upstairs with me, I put it on the dresser and finished getting ready for our night out. Cal had requested that I dress up and be ready by six p.m. I had plenty of time, but decided to go all out and curl my hair too. I couldn't remember the last time I was more excited about Valentine's Day, although my general consensus was that it was a stupid Hallmark holiday.

Hair and makeup were done and I pulled my red dress off the hanger. I only had a few dresses to choose from and I knew how much Cal liked that dress. It was the same one I wore to the auction, just a few months prior. Stepping into it, I heard his footsteps coming down the hall and turned to wait for him.

"Wow. You look amazing." He stood with his arms bracing the doorframe. His arms filled the long sleeves of the polo and he looked edible.

"Thank you." I pulled on the zipper and it stuck. "It's stuck, can you?"

"Absolutely."

He walked over and leaned in closer than necessary with his hands on the side zipper. Standing behind me, he nuzzled my neck as I inhaled deeply. He always smelled so good. He was nipping my neck as he worked the zipper loose. Turning my face toward his as he tugged on the zipper, it caught on my skin.

"Ow!"

"Shit. I'm sorry. Are you ok?" He pulled away as I checked my skin. There was no blood, but it sure did sting. "Jane, I'm so sorry."

Laughing, I said, "It's ok. I'll let you kiss it later." We managed to get the zipper up without any more skin abuse. "You should get ready or we'll be late."

He stepped back, grinning ear to ear. "What's wrong with what I'm wearing?" He held his arms up and showcased his outfit as I rolled my eyes at him. "Give me fifteen minutes."

I walked to the dresser as I said, "You have ten."

Running over, he swatted my ass, and ran into the closet before I could pay him back. I found the earrings he'd gotten me and placed them in my ears. Making my way downstairs, I checked my phone and paced the floor as I waited for him. Several minutes later he walked down the stairs. He was wearing a dress shirt and pants, but the shirt was unbuttoned on top and the sleeves were rolled up too. Biting my lip, I devoured him with my eyes.

When he left the bottom step, I put my hand in the air and motioned for him to turn around. "Tsk, tsk, tsk, Officer Charles. You clean up well." He obliged and strutted his stuff for me. Exaggerating his movements, my smile mirrored his as he moved closer to me.

"I hope you're up for dessert tonight." I raised my eyebrows at him wondering what he was insinuating. "Cuz I plan on dressing up your naked body with all kinds of yumminess and licking you clean."

I gulped and my mouth went dry as I asked, "What kind of yumminess?"

Smirking, he pointed toward the kitchen. I didn't see anything and he whispered, "In the fridge."

"Umm." I looked to the fridge and back to him before I walked over and opened the door. Chocolate syrup, honey, Redi-whip, fruit, and sprinkles sat inside. I giggled and looked back to him, "You're not getting this all over my sheets."

Walking over, with his eyes narrowed at me he replied, "Then I'll lay you out on the kitchen counter and eat you there."

"Don't make promises…"

Putting his finger to my lips, "I keep my promises." He leaned in and just when I thought he would kiss me, my eyes closed. "We're late."

Grabbing my hand, he pulled me toward the front door as I tried to regain my composure. I had a feeling it was going to be a long night, one I was sure I wouldn't soon forget.

We pulled up to valet at a fancy restaurant downtown and I looked at him. He saw the question in my eyes and just smiled. He hopped out of the truck and threw the keys at the valet before opening my door for me. I took his hand and got down as gracefully as I could. We walked inside and he gave his name to the host who then led us to a private room in back.

"Cal?" For him to get a private room—on Valentine's Day no less—had to have cost a fortune.

"Jane?" He just glared at me and I knew not to ask any more questions.

The room was small, but it was all ours. Champagne, along with two enormous chocolate covered strawberries, were waiting. The lighting was low and the room was filled with candles. It was the most romantic setting I'd ever been in. Cal handed the host something and the host nodded. I suddenly became nervous and couldn't help, but wonder if he was planning to propose. *Knock it off Jane.* I looked away, pretending not to see anything.

Music was playing and we were left alone in the room after the host said, "Your server will be here soon."

"Thank you." I turned back to Cal who had his hand out to me. "Come sit with me."

There was a small sofa in the room as well. He grabbed the glasses of champagne and handed me one as we sat down. I downed the glass, needing the alcohol to calm my nerves as he sipped his leisurely.

"Nervous?"

I glanced at him anxiously. "What? Why would I be nervous?"

He looked at me out of the corner of his eye as he said, "No reason."

He emptied his glass and set it down. I noticed that the music got a little louder and he got up and took me with him. Moving us to the small open space in the room, he pulled me close, with one hand resting on the small of my back while he held the other. I leaned into him and closed my eyes, burning the image of us into my memory.

He started whispering the lyrics in my ear. Meeting him back in October, I never would've taken him to be the thoughtful, hopeless romantic, country music listening, singing to his girlfriend and dancing with her under the stars type of guy. But he was. I think it was my favorite thing about him. *Who I Am With You* by Chris Young floated through the air as Cal sang it too.

"Baby doll, you've blessed me more than you could ever know. I never thought I'd find what I've found with you. I love you, Jane."

The tears were filling my eyes as he tipped my chin up. "Thank you."

Tilting his head, "For what?"

"Loving me. Unconditionally."

Snickering he said, "Loving you is the easy part."

Before I could ask what wasn't easy, his lips met mine. He took his time. He kissed me wholly and it was intoxicating. His hands ran over every part of my back, but it wasn't enough, I wanted more. Gripping the sides of his belt, I pulled him closer, his erection evident as it pressed into me. The sound of dishes being placed on the table startled me. Cal cupped my face and winked at me as the blush, at having been caught making out, spread over my face.

With my hand in his, he walked us over to the table and pulled out a chair for me. There was a plate with crab cakes sitting in the middle of the table. He moved his own chair from around the table and placed it next to mine. He joined our hands and we watched as the server refilled our glasses with champagne.

"Will there be anything else, Sir?"

"This is perfect. Thank you."

"Your entrée will be out shortly." He nodded and left the room.

"Sir, huh?"

"Fitting don't you think?"

Laughing, I said, "Don't get used to it. I prefer Officer Charles." He began cutting a piece of crab cake when I asked, "When did you order?"

"It's all taken care of. I placed our orders ahead of time."

I nodded, but wasn't sure what to make of it. No one had ever taken the liberty to order for me, except maybe my parents, and I wasn't sure how I felt about it. But I knew his heart was in the right place.

~ CALVIN ~

I GOT OUT of the shower and headed back to the bedroom. She wasn't there, thank God, and I quickly dressed and put the ring in my pocket. I made my way downstairs and when I reached the living room, she turned and raked her eyes over me while chewing on her lip. I laughed internally as I remembered her mother doing the same thing. They had similar mannerisms and it was endearing, though I wasn't about to tell her. Jane probably would've skinned me alive.

"Tsk, tsk, tsk, Officer Charles. You clean up well."

I put on a little show for her after she waved her index finger in the air. She wanted me to turn around. I paraded around the living room until her smile overtook her face. I couldn't stand the space between us and marched closer.

Her breath hitched as I said, "I hope you're up for dessert tonight." She lifted her eyebrows in response. "Cuz I plan on dressing up your naked body with all kinds of yumminess and licking you clean."

She almost stuttered as she inquired, "What kind of yumminess?"

Leaning in a little closer I cheesed it up and whispered, "In the fridge."

"Umm." She glanced between me and the fridge multiple times before walking over to it and pulling open the door.

On my way home I had picked up everything I could think of that I wanted to eat off her naked body. Chocolate syrup, honey, and Redi-whip came to mind first. Walking down the baking aisle I grabbed some sprinkles on a whim. And we couldn't have chocolate without some fruit. She stared at it all sitting in the fridge and let out the cutest little laugh.

Trying to be all serious she said, "You're not getting this all over my sheets."

Two could play that game. Squinting, I fired back, "Then I'll lay you out on the kitchen counter and eat you there."

"Don't make promises…"

Placing my finger on her lips to stop that luscious mouth of hers from tempting me further, I breathed out, "I keep my promises." I got as close to her as I could, teasing her with my kiss and just when she thought she'd get it, I pulled away. "We're late."

She was visibly disappointed, but we had somewhere to be. Latching on to her hand, we made our way out the door and to my truck. If everything worked out, by the end of the night she wouldn't be my girlfriend anymore. She'd be my fiancée. I wasn't sure when or how I'd do it, but the things I wanted to say to her had been replaying in my ear that whole week.

We made it to the restaurant and once inside I gave my name to the gentleman working the reservation desk. Thank God I had mentioned something in front of James and Smith. Apparently Delaney had redesigned the restaurant a while back and James was friends with the owner. He called in a favor and I was incredibly grateful. I wanted it to be a night to remember.

"Cal?" Jane was in shock and I knew what she was worried about.

"Jane?" I just stared her down and shook my head. Tonight, no price was too high, especially if it meant making her mine.

We were escorted to a private dining room in the back of the restaurant. Champagne and strawberries awaited us like I had requested. The ambiance of the room was perfect. Jane was busy taking in her surroundings when I handed the host the flash drive. I had insisted that we have our own music playing in the room and they had agreed. I patted my pocket to ensure the ring was still there and took a deep breath.

Once the flash drive was in his pocket he announced, "Your server will be here soon."

"Thank you." Jane's eyes met mine and I took her hand, asking her, "Come sit with me."

The quaint seating area was cozy and I took a glass in each hand. I sat down next to her and handed her one. She surprised me as she drank the glass right down. I sipped on mine and tried to calm my nerves. Why was I so nervous? She'd pleaded with me to ask her again. I knew she'd say yes and wanted to say yes. Maybe she'd caught on.

"Nervous?"

Her eyes darted to mine, "What? Why would I be nervous?"

Looking at her out of the corner of my eye I wondered if she suspected. "No reason."

Emptying my glass before placing it back on the table, I recognized my playlist beginning to play. I took her hand in mine, stood and pulled her close without asking if she wanted to dance or not. I was careful and held her hand that was on the same side as the ring in my pocket. I couldn't have her wondering what the hell I had in there.

Who I Am With You by Chris Young was coming through the speakers. The song playing was a newer song and I had identified with it since the first time I heard it. Jane had changed me or maybe she'd just uncovered something in me I didn't think would ever be found. I quietly sang the song to her as we held on to one another.

"Baby doll, you've blessed me more than you could ever know. I never thought I'd find what I've found with you. I love you, Jane."

The emotions were bubbling up in both of us. The evidence lingered in her tear soaked eyes as she said, "Thank you."

I crooked my head to the side wondering what she could possibly be thanking me for, "For what?"

"Loving me. Unconditionally."

"Loving you is the easy part." How could I not love her unconditionally?

I kissed her thoroughly, slowly, exhibiting more control than I wanted to. I would have loved nothing more than to take her to the floor and drink the rest of the champagne off her body. The pleasure was building in her too. Her hands latched on to my belt and tugged me closer. My cock throbbed, eager for some kind of release. I spotted the server coming in with our appetizer and watched as Jane blushed at being caught in the moment. Framing her face with my hands, I winked at her and led her to the table.

Our chairs were on opposite sides of the table and that was no good. I moved my chair to sit next to her and took my seat. Her hands were in her lap and I placed my hand on top of hers and laced our fingers together.

Our server refilled our glasses and asked, "Will there be anything else, Sir?"

"This is perfect. Thank you."

"Your entrée will be out shortly." He nodded and left the room.

"Sir, huh?"

"Fitting don't you think?"

Laughing she replied, "Don't get used to it. I prefer Officer Charles." As I cut a piece of crab cake, she asked, "When did you order?"

"It's all taken care of. I placed our orders ahead of time."

I momentarily hoped that it was ok that I had taken the liberty to order for her. I wanted us to have as much privacy as possible and knew that ordering ahead of time would also ensure we got the dishes I wanted us to. The crab cakes were delicious and it wasn't long before our salad was brought out.

When the server had left, I said, "I ordered the couples' dinner. There are more courses, but we share it all. I hope that's ok?"

"It's perfect, Cal. This whole night is perfect." She leaned in and kissed me softly. *She* was the perfect one.

My phone began vibrating and I tried ignoring it. When it was done it started right back up again. Sighing, I pulled it out and recognized Frank's number on the caller ID. He knew I was out tonight with Jane. Was he dense? It was Valentine's Day.

"Cal, it's ok if you have to answer it."

"No, not tonight." I was on a new case, but nothing would be going on with it, yet.

The phone started vibrating again and that's when I got worried. "Cal, please answer it."

"Sorry." I picked it up and asked Frank what was so important that he had to interrupt dinner.

The expression on my face must have tipped Jane off that something was horribly wrong. Frank began telling me that Melissa had been found naked, beaten, and possibly raped on the side of the road. Memories of Jane from that day flashed through my mind. I knew Melissa going in under cover could have consequences, but not like this. Dan had to be responsible and I thought I was going to lose my shit remembering that Dan had been dating my sister.

"Have them call Smith. That was the plan. Smith needs to know, he and James are the only ones she trusts." Jane's eyes got big as she squeezed my free hand. "Ok. Keep me posted. I'll be in touch in the morning, if I don't hear from you by then. Thanks, Frank." I ended the call and set the phone down on the table.

"Cal, what is it? What's wrong?"

How was she going to handle the details? Maybe I didn't need to give them to her. *Shit!* This was just my luck. I had to tell her. She at least needed to know that Melissa was fighting for her life.

Taking her hand in mine I said, "It's Melissa." Her eyes got big as she waited for me to say something more. "She's been attacked. She's in the hospital. It's bad."

I filled her in and answered any questions she had. The proposal wouldn't happen, not that night. She was visibly shaken at the news of Melissa and wanted to go to the hospital. I knew they weren't chummy by any means, but it just proved to me again at what a great person Jane was. The size of her heart rivaled only that of one other person I could think of. Cassidy. I was blessed to have them both in my life.

ten

~ CALVIN ~

Wᴇ ꜰɪɴɪꜱʜᴇᴅ ᴏᴜʀ ᴅɪɴɴᴇʀ, ʙᴜᴛ the mood was gone. She was visibly shaken by the news of what had happened to Melissa. The server brought me my flash drive back before we left and headed home. The proposal would have to wait. I didn't want any negativity around to ruin our moment. We drove home in silence as I rubbed small circles on her neck.

"Jane. You ok?"

She just shrugged her shoulders. "I feel like every time something good happens, something horrible happens." She sniffed and cried softly, "Are we doomed to a crazy roller coaster? Cuz if we are, I want off."

"Jane, there's no one else I want to ride this roller coaster with." She looked to me, doubt shadowing her eyes. "No one!"

"I just wish it wasn't so hard."

"It won't always be. It can't be." I prayed that I was right. We'd been through a lot in our short time together and there were more struggles to come. Eva's health was declining, the possible murder charges Jane was facing, and now Melissa.

Walking in the door, she made a beeline upstairs. After locking the door and hanging up my coat, I followed her. She was removing her jewelry and had already removed her heels. I watched as she took off her dress and laid it on the chair by the window. I loved watching her. She took the clip out of her hair and her long dark locks fell down her back. She was stunning and didn't even know it. Removing her bra, she threw on a sweatshirt and some shorts.

Spotting me, she smiled and walked over and wrapped her arms around my waist. "Want to watch a movie?" Her head was resting on my chest as I held her close.

"Sure. Go pick something out. I'm going to change."

Pulling back, she kissed me and said, "Ok. Don't be long."

When I knew it was safe, I pulled the ring out of my pocket and opened up the box. I was eager to see it on her finger. Taking a deep breath, I put it back in the safety of my drawer. Removing my clothes and pulling out some sweats, I spotted some paperwork on her side of the dresser and saw the San Francisco return address. Curiosity got the better of me and I opened it up. I didn't realize that she owned property there. It appeared that she had an interested buyer.

"Sorry, I should've told you." I turned to see her standing in the doorway. "It was my place with Derek. I have to get the apartment cleaned up so they can start showing it to potential buyers."

"It says he's behind on the payments."

"Yeah. Looks like he stopped paying the utilities and the HOA fees, I got them up to date. I was planning on talking to my boss about flying out in the next couple weeks."

What? She was going to Cali? "Can't you find someone to handle it for you?"

"Yes, but I need closure. Given the circumstances, I left a lot behind that I'd like to retrieve."

"Then I'm going with you."

She smiled and shook her head. "Cal, I'll be ok. You just started back to work."

"I have weeks of vacation stock piled. I'm going with you. Just let me know when."

"Ok. I'll have to check with Annie, too. I don't think the police would be too keen on me leaving the state right now."

"We'll figure it out."

~ JANE ~

I THINK I was in shock after I heard the news of Melissa. It was no secret that she wasn't my favorite person, but I would never wish upon her what had happened. I knew firsthand what she was experiencing. Cal said that she'd been drugged, beaten, raped and left for dead. It made me sick to my stomach.

When we got home, I changed my clothes and he did the same. We were planning to watch a movie and when I grew impatient waiting for him, I headed back upstairs to find him reading my letter from San Francisco. He was really cool about it all and insisted on going with me. I was glad to have his support because I knew it wouldn't be an easy trip for me to make, for numerous reasons.

We opted for a comedy and I put in one of my favorites, *Just Friends*. The movie was hilarious, but I wasn't able to keep from dozing off. When I woke, my head was gently lifting and rising to the rhythm of his breathing. He was on his back with me nestled between his legs. Closing my eyes, as my hand ran under his shirt, I fell back asleep.

I was moving and couldn't figure out what was going on. I shook the sleep and found Cal carrying me up the stairs.

"Put me down, you Oaf. You shouldn't be carrying me."

Snorting, "Oaf, huh? I'm fine. You weigh nothing."

I started to struggle and he let me go. Standing in front of him, he stared me down and before I knew it, I was over his shoulder.

"Calvin Charles!" I couldn't help, but giggle as he carried me to the bedroom and dropped me on the bed.

"Damn. You're heavy." My jaw dropped as he winked.

"Ass."

Pulling his shirt and lounge pants off, he crawled into bed in just his underwear. He yawned loudly as I pushed the covers down and crawled into bed.

"You wear too much to bed." He pulled on my shorts and sweatshirt. "How can you sleep with all that on?"

"Keeps me warm."

"Excuse me, that's what I'm for."

Sitting up on the edge of the bed, I removed my shorts and sweatshirt and grabbed a tank top before lying down next to him. I curled into his side as he sighed. "Better?"

"Much."

I threw my leg over his and let his warmth seep into me. He was snoring within moments.

I woke from another nightmare. This one was more violent than the others. I sat up, careful not to wake him, and headed downstairs for some water. Grabbing a glass, I got some water from the fridge and spotted the *yumminess* we didn't get a chance to utilize. I closed the fridge and walked to the front window, staring outside. It was another cold night and snow was lightly falling.

I decided to be a bit spontaneous and loaded up a tray with some of the fruit and toppings that Cal had picked out. Carrying it up the stairs, I tip-toed into the room, careful not to wake him. I placed the tray on my nightstand and looked over to him. He was sprawled out on his belly, in the middle of the bed—bed hog—the covers at his waist. *Perfect!*

I pulled the bottle of honey out of the warm water and dried it off. Straddling the backs of his legs, he groaned slightly, but didn't move. Testing the temperature of the honey, it was slightly warmer than my skin, and tasted it. It had cinnamon in it and it was delicious. I dribbled a small amount on to the base of his spine and bent over licking it clean. I drizzled more and made a trail further up his spine, before I began licking it off.

How was he sleeping through it? "Cal." I whispered his name as my lips kissed his shoulder blades. I went a little crazy with the honey and diligently licked up every drop.

He began moving slightly as I began sucking and licking on his neck. Sleepily he asked me, "What are you up to, woman?"

I just chuckled as I sat up and let more honey rain over his shoulders. He groaned as I sucked harder than necessary and my hands moved down his sides, massaging the muscles that lined his hips. When I was finished with his back, I moved lower and told him to roll over. He pulled his arms up and under his head and just stared at me before spotting the honey.

"Someone wanted some yumminess, huh?" Smiling mischievously, I nodded as I drizzled honey over his nipples. Leaning down, I took one into my mouth and as his hips rose up, he murmured, "Jane."

He was growing harder by the second as my abdomen brushed against him. Moving lower, I licked his honey and ink covered skin clean. I shifted and straddled his thigh, getting friction where I needed it most. He pressed his thigh into me and was rewarded with my moan. If he wasn't careful I'd ride his thigh, instead.

"Mmm, it's so good. You should try some."

I looked up at him as he stared at me, waiting for my next move. Pulling his underwear down, his cock bounced against his abs. The honey I poured flowed all over his shaft as I smiled wickedly. Without hesitation, I lavished my tongue all over him.

"Fucking shit, baby doll."

He tasted so good. I thought to myself that every blow job should come with a bottle of honey. He was hard, sticky, and pulsing in my mouth and I wanted more. Holding the base, I let a little more dribble over him before I began to suck him clean. Cal's thighs were clenched as I bobbed my mouth up and down his cock.

"I can't stand it. Jane, come here."

Slowly, I pulled my mouth off of him and stood on the bed. I removed my panties and my tank before walking closer to him. Standing above him, he pulled himself to a sitting position and kissed my thighs and hips as his hands squeezed my ass. With the honey still in my hand, I squeezed some on my skin, just below my belly button. Cal wasn't aware until some dripped down into the path he was kissing.

"More."

With the slightest hesitation, I put more on just above my always bare mound. He watched intently as it trickled down to my lips. Running his index finger through the honey and down to my clit before sticking it in his mouth.

"Delicious."

My legs were trembling as his mouth captured my clit. I grabbed the headboard as he threw my leg over his shoulder. His strong hands were holding on to my ass as I began to rock back and forth against his mouth. I couldn't take it anymore. Pulling away from him, I straddled his waist. His hands ran the length of my back as he pulled me closer. I squeezed a little drop of honey onto my tongue and his lips met mine immediately.

He tasted like me, with cinnamon honey on top. His throbbing cock was wedged between our bodies as I pressed into him. He reached for the nightstand drawer and I knew he was looking for a condom.

"Cal, I started the pill. I want to feel you, only you and me, nothing and nobody else. Ever."

"God, yes."

He lifted me and when he lowered me, it was onto him. We both sat still as my body clenched and stretched around him. Burying his head in my neck, he started to move his mouth over my quivering skin. I lifted up and glided back down his shaft. It felt so good, I did it again at once.

"Cal, I love you." He suckled my nipple while his fingers tweaked the other. "It feels so good."

"Where's the honey?"

Panting as I smirked, I held it up between us and drizzled more over my breasts. He licked up as much as he could without swallowing it and slammed his mouth to mine. My lips were swollen and tender as we lapped up our honey kiss. Our hips moved in succession for the ultimate contact.

"They're green, so very green."

I knew he was referring to my color-changing eyes as I felt my climax approaching at an intense pace. "Cal…"

"You're close. So. Am. I."

I shifted marginally as my body began to tense. "Don't…"

"I got you. Go crazy."

My nails dug into his shoulders as his hands guided my hips. I began crying out as his own movement became more determined. I found his mouth as my cries were swallowed up. My hands clenched on to him so tightly that I knew my knuckles would be white if I looked at them.

"Baby…" He couldn't finish his statement, instead he began to shake as I felt him burst into me. I clenched around him for optimum effect as he pleaded for me to stop. "Jane, stop that. I can't take it." I loosened my grip and slowly rocked my hips as he came down from his high.

We sat that way for longer than we should have. When we went to pull ourselves apart, our bodies were nearly stuck together. We both laughed at the sound that was made as we separated ourselves.

"I'd say a shower is in order."

As I stood, I agreed. "I think you're right." The comforter was honey free, or at least I hoped it was as I dragged it off the bed. I quickly whipped the sheets off and threw them in the laundry basket before we made our way to the shower. When our bodies were honey free, I put on clean ones.

eleven

~ CALVIN ~

THE NEXT WEEK I WAS MEETING with Smith, James, Paul and some other guys, who worked for them. They were making some progress on the video footage and had also gotten word that Melissa was awake. I knew Smith and James would get her to look at the footage as soon as they felt she was ready. We, ourselves, scoured it for hours and never spotted Dan or anyone else we recognized. Though, all of us were in the footage. We all prayed she recognized somebody or we were all screwed. A couple of suspicious people came up in the footage, but no one we could identify.

When I got home that night, I let Jane know that Melissa was awake. I also told her that we made great progress with the footage and if Melissa could identify someone, it should put Jane in the clear of murder charges.

"I'd like to go visit her." I just looked at her. "It's the right thing to do."

"I understand. I can go with you if you like."

Smiling, "No, it's ok. I'll go tomorrow when you're at work."

"Just be safe."

"Always."

WHEN JANE WENT to visit Melissa the next day, she'd been fast asleep. She left her a note and told her she'd stop by again in a few days. Saturday, we got the call from Smith that Melissa was starting to remember things. He informed us that he and James were headed to the hospital with the video footage.

After hanging up the phone I told her, "Melissa is starting to remember."

Her eyes got big and she took a deep breath. "Please let this be over soon. I hate this."

Pulling her to me I whispered, "I know, baby doll."

THE NEXT DAY we went up to the hospital. I stayed in the waiting room and Smith met me there while Jane went to see Melissa. He let me know that Paul had been spending a lot of his free time with Melissa. I wondered to myself if they had something going on. It would probably be a welcome distraction. Since finding out that Cass was now Mrs. Benedict, Paul was down in the dumps. He tried to brush it off that he wasn't feeling well, but I knew better.

"She remembers a lot and filled in the cops."

"Derek too?"

Smith knew what I meant, "I really think the charges will be dropped. Melissa has a clean record so there's no reason to doubt her story."

"God, I hope so. I'm not going to tell Jane. I don't want to get her hopes up. We need this done with."

"I know you do."

~ JANE ~

I WALKED TO her room and took a deep breath before knocking. We had a long history, maybe me more so than her. I hated her, had for a long time, since Jason's death. Blaming her for everything was easy to do when I was a teenage girl and mourning the death of my brother. Jason didn't start using until he started dating her—as far as I knew. What did it matter anymore? Jason had been gone for over fifteen years. God, I missed him.

Knocking, I cracked open the door and called her name, "Melissa? It's Jane. Can I come in?"

I saw her lean her head toward the doorway as she waved me in. She looked better than she had days prior. The abrasions to her face were healing nicely, but I knew the emotional wounds would probably never fully heal.

"I wanted to check in on you. I hope that's ok."

She nodded and I sat down the bag of goodies I brought her on the bed next to her. "What's this?"

"I thought you could use some distraction." I'd filled the bag with candy bars, trashy magazines, a crossword puzzle book, and a Sudoku book. I knew how boring hospital TV could be.

As she glanced through the bag, I caught half a smile spread across her face as she thanked me. I sat down in the chair next to her bed asking, "How are you doing?"

She began examining her fingernails and shrugged her shoulders. I wasn't prepared to see this side of her. In fact, I couldn't recall a time I'd ever seen her vulnerable. Her guard was always up and she was ready to cut a bitch without hesitation. I pulled the chair closer and laid my hand on her hand.

"Melissa. I'm so sorry. I know that what you went through wasn't the same as what I went through, but I understand."

Sniffling, she retorted, "No, it wasn't. Your prince charming saved you."

I was taken aback. I knew that she must've been referring to James. Did she really think he was her prince charming? In that moment, I felt sorry for her. She'd spent so long trying to capture my cousin's attention that she quite possibly missed out on something or someone who would love her for her.

"Melissa, Cal almost died."

"I know, but if he hadn't gone in search of you…"

She was right. Had Cal just let me go, I probably would've died trying to get away from Derek. "Melissa, I don't know what to say about James."

"You don't have to say anything. He's not the one for me. I knew it a long time ago, before Cassidy came along, but I just couldn't let him go." Her eyes glanced mine for a second. "It's silly, I know."

"It's not silly. The heart is a tricky thing. If anyone knows that, I do." I smiled at her and let out a big breath. "He and Cassidy really are great together. She's wonderful—but that's probably the last thing you want to hear."

She laughed at that. "Yeah, well. I'm still a woman scorned, though I have no right to be." We chatted a little while longer, until she became drowsy. I got up to leave and she grabbed my hand. "I told the police everything I could. I know you didn't kill Derek."

"Thank you. I'm just glad you're going to be ok."

"Thank you for coming."

"Of course. Seriously, if you need anything, please call me."

She just nodded at me and I headed out of the room. I said a silent prayer all the way to the waiting room. I hoped with everything I had, that what she told the cops was enough to take the suspicion off of me.

CAL CAME HOME from work early the next day. He barreled through the front door so abruptly that I about jumped out of my skin, thinking someone busted it down.

"Jane, Jane, baby. Where are you?"

"Cal? What's wrong?" I was standing on the top of the stairs looking down to him. He was beaming.

"Jane, it's over."

My heart and stomach flipped over one another, not wanting to get my hopes up. "What's over? What are you talking about?"

Bounding up the stairs, two at a time, he wrapped his arms around my waist and gave me a big hug. "The statement Melissa gave has placed the blame elsewhere. No charges will be filed against you. You're free. I talked to Annie, too. It's over."

I stopped breathing and closed my eyes as I rested my cheek against his neck. "It's over?"

"It's over!"

I wrapped my legs around him, not wanting to let go. I was so overcome with so many different emotions, I didn't know whether to laugh or cry. So, I did both. Certain that I looked and sounded ridiculous, but he didn't seem to notice. When I finally let him pry my body off of his, I saw tears of joy swimming in his own eyes.

"I love you, Cal."

"I love you! You should call your parents."

That put a huge smile on my face. I ran to the bedroom and grabbed my phone. Dialing my mom, I sat on the bed and waited for her to answer.

"Mom, are you sitting down?"

"Jane, what's going on now?"

"Nothing bad! It's the opposite."

"Well don't keep me waiting in suspense. What is it?"

"It's over, I'm free. A witness came forward and they won't be pressing any charges against me." She didn't say anything. "Mom?" I heard her sniffles as she denied that she was crying.

"You two should come over for dinner. This calls for a celebration."

"Hang on." I looked to Cal and asked, "Can we do dinner with Mom tonight?" He nodded and smiled. "Sounds good, mom. We'll be over in a couple hours."

"Alright dear. I'll call your father and tell him the good news."

"Is he out of town again?"

"Yes, West Coast."

That reminded me. I had to book my flight to San Francisco. "Ok. We'll be over later." I disconnected the call and looked to Cal. "That offer still good for going to Cali with me?"

"Absolutely. Boss said I just need to notify him a few days in advance."

"Perfect." I pulled my laptop off the night stand and started searching for flights. "You're sure you can take a week?"

"Yup. What about you?"

"Yes. Sylvia wasn't happy, but I volunteered to be on call for a while, until I'm back on the normal rotation!" He sat down next to me as I said, "There's a flight next Monday, returning that Friday."

"Let's do it."

We had dinner that night with my mom. Nothing too exciting happened. We talked about my Aunt Eva and her declining health.

"Should I wait to go out of town?" I asked nervously as Cal squeezed my hand.

"Honey, I think you'll be fine. It's just a few days and she's been really good these past few weeks."

I nodded in approval, but being in the medical industry, I knew how quickly the tables could be turned. "I'll go see her before we leave."

"That's a great idea."

"You know she'd love to see you." Mom smiled at us.

Shortly after, we left her to her charity work and headed home. We were driving along when I realized he wasn't headed toward home, but toward our back road. I stared at his profile, willing him to look at me. When he did, he had that huge cheesy grin on his face. Reaching for the stereo, he picked a song to play.

Cruise by Florida Georgia Line filled the cab of the truck. He rolled the windows down and started singing.

"Cal! It's freezing out." He laughed as he rolled them back up, but kept on singing. It wasn't long before he pulled into our little alcove and I started the song over.

We were singing the song to each other and laughed when we sang the wrong words or hit a wrong note. He slid out of the truck and jogged over to my side and opened my door. It was cold out, but we'd be ok for a few minutes. We climbed into the bed of his truck, with the windows open so the music filled the air. He spun me around as we danced and sang on our own personal stage.

The song ended and we were still laughing and I was trying to catch my breath. Our breath formed a slight fog between us as a slow song came on next. He outstretched his hand to me and I eagerly took it.

"*Must Be Doin' Something Right* by Billy Currington."

"Hmm...I think you're trying to put the moves on me again, Officer Charles."

"Maybe." His hand pulled my head closer as he kissed my head.

We danced to the song and the joy that filled me had me elated. It was over. I wasn't going to be charged with Derek's murder and Cal and I could move on with our lives. Preferably a life together. I briefly thought about our dinner on Valentine's Day and wondered if he was planning to propose that night. I put it in the back of my brain. If it was going to happen, it would happen. I just had to be patient. I wasn't going anywhere and he'd told me over and over that neither was he.

I had never wanted to freeze time so badly like I did at that night. Everything seemed to be falling into place. I knew how lucky I was that we were both alive and together. The song ended and I didn't want to let go. A tremor passed over my body from the cold.

"You're cold. We should get going. We can continue this at home."

Squeezing him tighter, I pleaded, "Just a few more. I don't want to forget this moment."

"Mmm. Do you want to pick the song?"

I jerked my head up and smiled as I squealed, "Yes!" I leapt out of the bed of the truck and climbed back in the cab. He was sticking his head through the open slider in back, trying to see what song I'd pick. "Hey! No peeking!" Laughing, he pulled his head out and sat on the edge of the bed and waited while I scrolled through my songs on my 'CAL' playlist.

I picked the song *My Kind of Love* by Emeli Sande. As it started playing I headed to the back of the truck. He offered me his hand as I climbed back up. He didn't say anything, just began dancing with me slowly.

I took in some deep breaths as the smell of winter and Cal's cologne filled me. It was all consuming as my head began to feel heavy from his heady scent. I made a declaration when the song was over.

"I want this to become a ritual for us."

He looked at me curiously. "What do you mean?"

"This. Us in the dark, under the stars, dancing as we listen to songs we love."

Leaning down, he kissed me and it wasn't long before we were tugging and pulling on each other, trying to get closer. He backed me up against the cab and lowered himself slightly so that his groin was pressed tight against me. Shifting my hips, the little burst of pleasure traveled through me.

"Cal."

"Shh. And, you have a deal." He was kissing down my neck. "This will be our ritual. If I ever forget just smack me."

I was smiling and moaning at the delight of his whiskers against my skin. "And you have to keep the facial hair."

"Oh, do I?"

"Yes, or the deal's off."

He sighed, "If you insist."

twelve

~ CALVIN ~

"Jane, are you ready?"

She was pacing the bedroom, talking to herself. I smiled and listened as she checked off her mental to-do list. Our suitcases were waiting by the front door. Paul had offered to drive us to the airport, but we passed.

"Ok. I think I have everything." She smiled and raised her eyebrows. "Let's do this!"

We got to the airport and checked one bag before heading to our terminal. When it came time to board, she stood when they announced first class boarding.

"Jane?"

Shrugging her shoulders. "I could've taken the Benedict jet, but since you wouldn't let me, first class is the next best thing."

I rolled my eyes at her and shook my head. I'd never flown first class before and was surprised at how comfortable the seating actually was. We spent the flight chatting about nothing in particular and listening to music. She read some and looked over the paperwork for the apartment. With the help of some friends of hers from San Francisco, she'd lined up cleaners and movers.

We landed around lunch time and after we collected our bag, and got our rental car, we were off. I'd never been to California and was enjoying the scenery as she drove. We stopped for lunch at one of her favorite places. It was a little French café and she opted to sit outside. The weather was tolerable considering the cold climate we had been in that morning.

"Do you want to check in to the hotel or go to the apartment first?" We were almost done with our meals and she averted her eyes and I knew she was thinking about it.

"I think I want to just get it over with. The hotel is reserved so we don't have to worry about checking in right away." She made eye contact and I smiled my approval. "Besides, I'd like to show you some of the sights if time allows."

"I'd love that."

I paid for lunch, much to her chagrin and we got back in the car. She drove a few blocks and pulled into a parking spot. She was staring out her window and I followed her gaze. Gently, I squeezed her hand and she forced a smile before getting out of the car.

"I have to stop by the manager's office first. I don't have a key. I left it when, well, when I left."

"Ok. Just tell me what you need me to do." She reached for my hand as we headed to the office.

There wasn't much of a fuss in the manager's office. The old woman seemed oblivious to the turmoil Derek had caused and acted annoyed, but handed over a key after confirming Jane had gotten all the balances paid and up to date. Jane confirmed she'd turn it back in when the apartment was ready for showings.

We rode the elevator up a couple floors and I followed her down the hall. Her demeanor had completely changed. I was beginning to think that I should've insisted she hire someone to handle collecting her things. I only prayed it all went smoothly and that she wouldn't regret coming.

Her hand was shaking as she tried to put the key in the lock. "Jane. You don't have to do this."

She looked to me with glassy eyes. "Yes, yes I do."

"Ok." I took the key from her and opened the door for her.

What I saw wasn't what I expected. The place looked like it had been completely ransacked. I immediately shielded her with my body as I scanned the place.

With no weapon I shouted, "Police!" Holding perfectly still, I heard nothing. The place was empty. Derek must've trashed the place before he left town after Jane.

I let her pass as she walked through slowly, taking in what was left of her old life. The apartment was in shambles. We had our work cut out for us. I followed her around cautiously. It was a nice place, or had been before it was trashed. It was big, too. I tried to not become self-conscious about how small and basic my place was. She wasn't materialistic, but she was used to more than I was able to give her. She stopped at a doorway and I realized it was the bedroom.

"I can't go in there. Not yet."

Placing my hands on her shoulders I said, "Its fine. I'll take care of it."

Eventually she found some cleaning supplies and garbage bags. We had several garbage bags filled and were starting to make piles of what was to be donated, sold, and what she wanted to take back home. We both looked to each other when there was a knock on the door.

"Jane. It's Becky."

A huge smile spread across her face. "She's a friend from work."

I walked to the door and opened it as Jane came over. They embraced as Becky said, "I couldn't wait for you to call. I had to see if you were here." They separated as Becky took in the place. "Jesus. He left it this way?"

Shrugging her shoulders Jane just said, "You should've seen it a couple hours ago."

Becky looked to me and back to Jane as she asked, "Umm, who's this?" Her tone was telling and I couldn't help but chuckle.

"Becky, this is Cal. Cal, this is Becky." I put my hand out and she hugged me instead.

"Jane, your description didn't do him justice."

"Hi, Becky. I'm Calvin, Cal, either works."

"Nice to meet you."

"Likewise."

Becky dove right in with us and we got some more work done. A couple hours later, Becky mentioned that she was famished and we all agreed. There wasn't any food in the apartment so we were out of luck.

"Why don't you girls go grab something to eat and I'll keep working here?"

Becky smiled brightly at both of us and asked, "Is he for real?"

Jane laughed and said, "He is and he's all mine." She walked to me and asked, "Are you sure?" I nodded, knowing they had some catching up to do. "Ok. We'll pick up a pizza and some drinks and bring it back."

"That's fine, but you can just bring me something back if you want. It's no big deal. I'll be fine."

She kissed me, "Ok. We won't be long."

I gathered the full bags and put them down the garbage shoot that

Jane had pointed out in the hallway. I found an iPod dock and attached my phone to listen to some music. There wasn't much more for me to do in the living room so I headed toward the bedroom.

I knew she wasn't ready to deal with it yet. I figured I could deal with the mess to make it easier for her later on. Another bag of garbage was almost full. I set it down and headed to the closet. She'd mentioned wanting to donate all his clothes so I bagged them up and carried them to the donation pile in the living room.

Returning to the bedroom closet, which was almost empty, except for Jane's items, I spotted a shoebox in the corner. My suspicions got the better of me and I picked it up and pulled the lid off. It appeared to be a box of keepsakes, but I wasn't sure if they were Jane's or Derek's. Spotting a small tan bi-fold card, I picked it up. On the other side 'My Baby' was printed on it. My stomach dropped.

Setting the box down, I took the card and sat on the bed as my mind began racing. Opening the bi-fold, a couple black and white photos stared back at me. Jane's first and last name were up at the top along with her birthdate. There were two pictures stapled to the card. One had the word 'Baby' with an arrow pointing to the small object in the middle of the picture. The other didn't have any words on it, just another image similar to the first one. In Jane's handwriting it said '8wks, 4days'.

Jane *had* been pregnant. I looked at the date on the card and it was from the previous May. Jane had fled back home in June. I tried doing the math in my head, but my brain wouldn't function. I was an idiot. All those times Jane tried talking to me or shut down on me. Was she trying to tell me about the baby? But there wasn't a baby. I didn't put too much thought into what had happened. I had a pretty good idea myself about what had happened.

~ JANE ~

I GOT IN BECKY'S car as we drove toward our favorite pizza joint. "So, spill it. How'd you meet him? He's hot!"

Chuckling, I replied, "Actually, he's the brother of my cousin's girlfriend. Well, actually his wife now. So he's my cousin's brother-in-law." I looked to her and she raised her eyebrows. "Is that weird?"

"Hell no. Not when he's that hot. Might be awkward if you guys break up, or they do."

"Hold your tongue." We both laughed as I said, "I don't see that happening. He's totally smitten with her and she's great."

"Uh, so is Cal! It's obvious. Hell, I'm smitten with him!" We were sitting, waiting for our pizza when she asked, "Seriously. He's a good guy right?"

It dawned on me that she knew very little about what had happened in December. "He took a bullet for me. He's a good guy." I filled her in on the details she didn't know.

"Jane, does he know what you lost?"

I just shook my head. "Not everything."

"Jane, you should tell him."

"I know."

Becky was still single and loving playing the field. Part of me envied her freedom, but I wouldn't trade Cal for anything. Cal wasn't suffocating like Derek was. Cal loved me for me and didn't want to change me. We stopped by a local market and picked up some bottles of water, a bottle of wine, and some snacks.

We got back to the apartment and Cal wasn't in the living room. "Give me a minute." I set the pizza on the counter and Becky put the other bags down as well and waved me on.

I found him in the bedroom. He'd made a lot of progress in the time Becky and I were gone. He was sitting on the bed and looking at something in his hand. As I circled the bed I saw what he was holding and my stomach convulsed. Well, he knew all my secrets now. I'd forgotten about the ultrasound image and he'd found it.

His head was resting on one hand that was propped up on his knee, as the other held the picture between his legs. He looked perplexed and he had every right to be. I sat down next to him, unsure what I should say or do and scared to death that it might change how he looked at me.

"Cal?" He lifted his eyes to mine and he was crying. It was like a punch to the gut. I tried to hold back the tears, but it was impossible. My throat began to ache as the tears began rolling down my cheeks. "I was so happy, convinced it was a boy. It was a surprise and I thought that Derek would be happy."

"Jane. You lost the baby because of him, didn't you?"

I couldn't physically say the words, but he knew the answer. He wrapped his arms around me and pulled me to his lap. "Baby doll, I'm so sorry." I let the tears flow as he soothed me. "It all makes sense now."

"I'm sorry I didn't tell you. It was just, so, personal. Nobody knows except you and Becky."

"Your mom?"

"No."

"Jane. I wish you would've told me sooner, but it doesn't change anything. I love you. Would've loved you had I met you and you were pregnant or had a baby on your hip."

I smiled at that and knew it was true. Cal didn't care about my baggage, never had, and never would. I fell in love with him just a little bit more after that.

"Should I leave you two alone?"

Her words rang down the hall. I giggled as we were reminded that Becky was still there. "Becky's waiting with dinner."

"Good. I'm starving."

thirteen

~ JANE ~

We were lying in bed that night at the hotel. It felt later than it was due to the time difference and we were both exhausted. My head was on his shoulder as I started to drift off.

"Jane, you know you can trust me right? With anything."

I knew I could, but he didn't know that. I'd hindered his faith of my faith in him because I had kept so much from him. "I know. I'm sorry." Lifting my head I looked to his face. "There isn't any more. I know that may be hard to believe, but it's true."

He smiled wickedly and I wondered what was stirring in that brain of his. "Hmm, so when did you lose your virginity?"

Laughing, I smacked his arm. "It's a boring story. I was seventeen and it was after Prom."

"How textbook of you."

"Yeah, what about you?"

"High school after a football game. I was seventeen, too."

"Hmm. Well, I bet you were hot then, too."

"I'll let you believe that!"

WE SPENT THE whole next day working in the apartment. Becky was there most of the day and her flavor of the month came and helped once he was out of work. The realtor had stopped by and I decided to offer it for sale as partially furnished. It would save us a lot of time and hassle that way. I didn't have very many belongings that I wasn't willing to part with. The clothes I wanted to keep were boxed up and ready to be shipped.

Cleaners were coming in the morning to scrub the place down and then the realtor would help stage the place. Cal was in the office boxing up the filing cabinet. Derek had a full cabinet dedicated to work stuff. I wasn't sure what to do with it. Deciding to call his old secretary, I asked her.

"Hey Leslie, its Jane, Jane Whitford."

"Oh, my goodness. Jane! How are you?"

"I'm good. Listen, I'm packing up Derek's apartment and there are work files here. I'm not sure what to do with them."

I listened intently as she told me that there had been suspicion of foul play on Derek's part. She said that it would be greatly appreciated if I dropped off the files. Now I was nervous and not sure what I should do.

"Ok. Thank you Leslie. I'll be in touch." After disconnecting the call, Cal picked up on my concern.

"What's wrong, babe?"

"Derek was under investigation by HR at his work. They knew a bunch of his files were missing. But he left and now he's dead, I don't know what to do."

"Why don't you call Annie? I'm sure she could help point you in the right direction."

"Good point. Ok." I pulled up Annie's number and waited for her to answer. "Hey Annie. I have a question."

Annie advised that I hand over all physical documents or belongings that I suspected were property of Derek's former employer. His personal computer she advised that I keep and take back home. I was irritated that I was getting mixed up in more of his drama, but I knew his family wouldn't take care of it. He was close to his mom, but she was a train wreck and I wasn't about to involve her if I didn't need to.

We loaded up the last of the boxes to get shipped home after the local homeless shelter picked up my donations. I signed the necessary paperwork in the office and with my realtor. Closing should be easy once an offer was made. The day was almost over, but now Cal and I had a couple days to ourselves. I really wanted to spend some one on one time with him, our troubles now behind us.

~ CALVIN ~

SOMEHOW I WAS more in love with her than ever. Something about knowing she had carried a life inside her, and she was excited about it, pulled at a part of me I didn't know had existed. I wanted her to be the mother of my kids, I wanted to grow old with her, I wanted her.

We'd spent all day Tuesday busting ass so we could get the hell out of that place. She promised she didn't have any more secrets, the lost pregnancy the only remaining untold story. I tried to imagine myself in her shoes and I just couldn't do it. I think I would've murdered Derek in his sleep if I had been her.

We were sitting in the hotel with carryout that evening, talking about what to do Wednesday and Thursday. "We don't have to make plans. We can just drive and see where we end up."

She smiled at me. "I'm totally fine with that. We don't have to be at the airport until Friday morning."

"Deal."

When she was asleep, I went through my things and found the ring. I wasn't sure why I brought it, but I had. Pulling up the laptop, I did some research and found where I wanted to go. She could think it was unplanned, but I would know better.

When I woke her the next morning, she was a little put off. "Come on, baby doll. Time to go."

"I thought we were taking it easy, no plans."

"I lied. Come on."

She scowled at me all the way into the shower. We checked out of the hotel and got in the car.

"So, where to, Officer Charles?"

I punched in the address to where we were headed in my GPS app. "Follow the directions."

It was a beautiful day and a little warmer than I thought it would be. We pulled into the Napa Valley and she asked where we were going.

"Just follow the directions, woman." I winked at her as she smacked my arm. She pulled into the parking lot and parked the car. "Come on." We got out of the car and I met her and suggested, "How about some wine tasting and shopping?"

She smiled, "That sounds wonderful." She grabbed a sweater and her purse before we started walking.

We spent most of the afternoon getting tipsy and walking to different wine tasting bars. Her cheeks were flushed from the alcohol and I was feeling it too. She'd found a couple different bottles that she liked and ordered some cases to have shipped home.

We stumbled upon a coffee shop and decided some caffeine was in order for both of us. We sat and drank our coffee, and enjoyed some pastries while we people watched.

When she was done with her snack I said, "We can check in now."

"Check in? Where?" I pointed across the street and she turned her head toward the popular bed and breakfast. "Really!" She looked back to me, beaming. "I've heard wonderful things about them."

"I booked us a room for tonight and tomorrow. We can stay in bed all day if you want."

She got up from her seat and plopped down in my lap. "I love you. You're amazing." She kissed me quickly before jumping back up and pulling me toward the door.

We grabbed our luggage and headed into the hotel. The décor was very nice and Jane couldn't stop looking around. I got us checked in while she perused the lobby. I made some other arrangements to surprise her before we headed up to our room.

"Oh, Cal. It's really nice."

The room had a beautiful king sized bed sprawled in the middle of the room. A small living area was in the corner with a couch, TV, and coffee table. The dining area sat in front of the balcony window. She opened the balcony door and spotted a small Jacuzzi hidden in the corner.

"Oh, my God! This is amazing." Turning back to me, "How long have you had this planned?"

"I'll never tell." I wasn't about to tell her that I had only called a day ahead of time and got lucky. The clerk at the hotel had recommended the place and he was right. It was just what we needed. "Did you bring a swim suit?" She shook her head. "Too bad. You won't need it."

"Cal, it's out in the open."

I looked around and replied, "There's no one above us or beside us and the people below us can't see a thing with all the trees. You, me, and that hot tub, naked. It's going to happen!"

"I might have to arrest you for indecent exposure, Officer."

"Not if I arrest you first!"

We took a short nap and when she woke up, I asked if she wanted to do room service or head down to the restaurant. She opted for the restaurant so we got ready and headed down. That worked for me. Tomorrow would be the day.

Dinner was better than we thought it would be and we both ate way too much. As we headed back to our room, I asked for a bottle of dessert wine and fresh fruit to be sent up to our room in an hour or two. Jane tried objecting, telling me I was doing too much, but I got my way.

She walked into the room telling me that she was going to help cover the cost, when I yanked her back against me. "You'll do no such thing. I can afford to spoil you now and then."

Before she could say anything more, I captured her mouth and held her face in my hands. She moaned her delight and gripped the sides of my shirt. She didn't hesitate to pull it out of my pants so she could run her hands underneath. Her hands were slightly cool to the touch as she left her mark on my abs.

"Stay right there." I pulled away and put some music on.

She rolled her eyes at me and sarcastically said, "Player."

"Only for you!" She laughed at that while I fiddled with my phone to find a song. "Any requests?"

"Surprise me! And, it better not be country." She couldn't contain her laughter when I glared at her.

In that moment I knew exactly what song to play, just to convince her I listened to more than *just* country. *More of You* by The Goo Goo Dolls started playing. I sauntered back over to her as she scoured her eyes over me.

"I'm impressed. You actually know something other than country."

"Watch it, woman." I stood a few feet from her and motioned her to come closer.

She lifted her chin before she tilted her head at me. Pulling off her sweater, she dropped it on the floor before walking closer. "Is there something you wanted?"

"Yup. I know exactly what I want." I bent down and wrapped my arms around her hips and picked her up. She leaned her head down and kissed my lips. "I want you naked in that hot tub. But first, I'm going down on you."

She moaned in approval before I set her back down. I didn't waste any time removing her clothes before I sprawled her out on top of the bed. It was beautiful how she spread herself out for me, completely trusting and wanting. I didn't hesitate and tended to my task with diligence.

"Shit. You're going right for it."

I raised my eyes and found her gazing down at me, propped up on her elbows, as she watched me tongue her pussy. Her clit was already swollen and she was wetter than I thought she'd be.

"You're already wet for me, baby doll." She responded with an incoherent groan. "I think you like when I talk to you. Is that pussy ready for me?"

"Yes, please."

"I like it when you ask nicely."

"Please, stop talking."

I chuckled and resumed licking and sucking on her as my fingers entered her. I used sweeping circles to drive her over the edge. She came quick and hard. I was beaming with pride as she tried to shove my head out from between her legs.

"Don't go to sleep." She opened one eye and stared at me. "Hot tub. Let's go."

I stepped out on to the deck and took the lid off and turned the jets on. She climbed off the bed and I smirked as she stumbled toward the deck. There was a knock on the door and she stopped in her tracks.

"Get in. I'll be right there."

"Shit, its cold out here."

"Get in the hot tub, Jane!"

I opened the door and found a cart with the dessert wine on ice, a corkscrew, and fresh fruit waiting for me. The room service attendant was nowhere to be seen. Pushing the cart into the room, I heard her in the bathroom.

"Jane, what are you doing?"

She came walking out in a robe and held up the other. "It's freezing out there." Looking to the tray she just shook her head. "Hurry up!"

fourteen

~ JANE ~

I TOOK THE ROBE OFF AND GAVE him a show as I walked out to the hot tub. I set the robes down on a chair by the hot tub and climbed on in. It had been a perfect day and I knew it couldn't get any better. He walked up, butt-ass naked, carrying a tray. He set it down and handed me two glasses filled with wine. Picking up a smaller tray covered with fruit, he placed that on the edge of the tub before climbing in.

He sat down and pulled a strawberry off the tray and held it out for me. As I moved closer, I opened my mouth before he gave me a bite. He ate the other half as I handed him his glass. The sky was dark, but the stars were very prominent. It was a gorgeous night. I curled into his side and placed my legs across his lap.

"Thank you for today. It's been wonderful."

"Just wait. Tomorrow will be even better." He kissed my temple.

"Oh, will it? I can't wait to see what you have up your sleeve."

I turned my gaze toward his as he pushed some hair behind my ear. His fingers trailed over my face lovingly as I leaned in closer. He threw back the rest of his wine and set the glass down before pulling me into his lap. I downed the rest of my wine as well and discarded the glass.

We made love in the hot tub as he whispered sweet nothings to me. The wine and heat of the water was getting to me and so was the orgasm. He helped me climb out and the minute the cold air hit our bodies, we grabbed our robes and ran into the warmth of our room. Once we both had our robes on securely, he went back to the deck, closed up the hot tub, and brought in our glasses and tray.

I was picking up our clothes when he tried to stop me from grabbing his jeans. I felt something bulky in his pants pocket and reached my hand in to see what it was without thinking. The square velvet box surprised me. I was speechless. Time stood still and the only thing I could hear was my heart beating and the song that was playing. *Don't You Wanna Stay* by Jason Aldean and Kelly Clarkson was a beautiful song and there was no doubt that my answer was yes to every question the song asked.

"Cal..." He was standing there just looking at me and the velvet box. He took a deep breath and came a little closer. "I'm sorry, I..." He took the box and pants from me. He discarded the pants and stared at me for a moment before raking his hands over his face. I'd ruined it. AGAIN. "I ruined it."

His head whipped up as he took my hands in his. "No, you didn't ruin it. It's fitting really. I've planned three proposals just for them all to be messed up." Three proposals? What was he talking about? "Maybe this is how it's supposed to happen."

He got down on one knee and looked up at me after he opened the box. The ring was beautiful, but I couldn't keep my eyes off of him. We must have looked ridiculous, there in bath robes, in the middle of a hotel room. It was perfect.

"Jane. I promised you that I'd ask you again. Well, again is apparently now."

My free hand was clutching my chest as I listened to his words. It was different than the last time. There was no fear, no worry, and no trepidation about the things he didn't know, the things I hadn't revealed. He knew it all. I was so happy and knew that tears were filling my eyes. I bit my lip to keep from shouting YES before he finished asking.

"I want to spend my life with you and only you. I want to shout on rooftops that you belong to me." That had me giggling as he said, "I want you to have my babies. I want to travel the world with you. I want to be your everything, just like you're mine. Jane, will you marry me."

I was practically jumping up and down as I cried out, "You're my everything, too. Yes. I'll marry you." Before he could put the ring on my finger, I flung myself in his arms. We laughed and cried as we kissed each other senseless.

He finally pulled away and said, "Try it on." My hand was shaking as I put it in front of him. Taking my hand, he slid the ring over my finger.

"It's perfect." It fit perfectly and it was stunning. He had great taste or he had help.

"You're sure you like it?"

"Yes. I love it. I love you."

We were lying in bed, tangled in the sheets, and I was admiring my ring again. I remembered him saying something about having planned three proposals and had to ask.

"What did you mean by three proposals?"

He explained how he had planned to propose on Valentine's Day—number two—but then we got the call about Melissa. "The third was that I was going to propose at dinner tomorrow, here in the room. But you ruined that."

I smacked his belly protesting, "I said I was sorry."

"I'm kidding! You didn't ruin it. It's perfect just the way it happened." Holding me close, he asked, "Have you thought about when you'd like to get married?"

His question surprised me a little, but I wasn't really sure. Yes, I'd dreamt of my wedding since I was a little girl, but wasn't sold on the time of year. "Um, I'm not sure. You?"

"I'd marry you tomorrow if I thought that was what you wanted."

"My mother would kill me. And I want a wedding. I still can't believe James and Cassidy eloped the way they did."

"Don't get me started." I looked to him as he began ranting about the whole situation. "She's been dreaming of a big wedding since she was a little girl, I would know. She doesn't even have a ring. What the hell is wrong with that cousin of yours?"

"They love each other. Isn't that the important thing? Dreams can change."

He sighed, "Yes, but she deserves more. She'll lie till she's blue in the face that eloping was what she wanted. She wants the big party, a dress, my dad giving her away, and a ring. I mean, she plans weddings for a living. She loves it. She dreams it."

I felt sorry for Cassidy in that moment. Cal was right, he had to be. Maybe I needed to have a talk with James. "Not all guys are as romantic and over the top like you."

"HA! I don't think any of my previous *girlfriends* would agree with that statement."

That surprised me a little. I had just assumed that was how he was. "Why not?"

He shrugged his shoulders. "Romance was never important to me, not until you. Dreams change." He looked at me and seemed to sense the question I was thinking. "I almost lost you and I want to take advantage of every moment. I'll never stop trying to surprise you, make you smile, make you fall harder. I want you to have memories to recount for a lifetime."

He was amazing. "You're amazing. I have plenty of memories."

"You're not so bad yourself." Shortly after that, we fell asleep.

I was woken up by a knock on the door. Looking to the clock I saw that it was after eight a.m. Breakfast had arrived. I rolled the cart into the room and my stomach responded immediately to the aroma filling the air. Pushing it over to the small dining table in front of the deck, I pushed back the curtains and let the sun shine in.

Climbing on the bed, with a piece of bacon in my hand, I ran it under Cal's nose to help rouse him. "Cal, wake up. Breakfast is here." I nibbled his ear as I said it again and he started groaning.

I sat up as he rolled over and stretched his arms up above his head. "Breakfast here?"

I just nodded and took a bite of the bacon. "Yup, and it's delicious!" He reached for me, but I jumped off the bed before he could get me. "Come on, lover."

He climbed out of bed and I nibbled my bacon as I watched his naked figure glide around the room. Pulling some underwear out of the suitcase, he started to put it on when he caught me pouting. He looked much better naked.

"See something you like?"

I waggled my brows and demanded, "No shirt."

He dropped the t-shirt he'd grabbed and joined me at the dining table. "How come you get to wear a shirt?" I laughed as he winked at me. I had put on his discarded shirt from the night before.

"So, I was thinking about a summer wedding."

Smiling brightly, "I knew you had something in mind." He shoved some bacon in his mouth before saying, "Better get a move on. It's already March!"

I started laughing. He was crazy if he thought I could plan a wedding in a few months. "Um, *next* summer."

"What? Why? Jane, don't make me wait another year."

"Do you have any idea how much planning there is to do?"

"Yup and I'm sure Cass can help. She's got connections. She can make it happen."

I pondered that for a moment. Deep down I knew I didn't want to wait another year. "Give me a few minutes. I need to process this." He just chuckled as we ate our breakfast.

I was leaning back, full of French toast, bacon, eggs, and fruit. Cal was drinking some orange juice and was staring me down. I stared right back wondering what he was thinking about. He was challenging me and wouldn't give up.

"What about a Fall wedding?" He shook his head. "Oh, my God. You're relentless." I massaged my temples and pondered the idea of a summer wedding. "I could maybe do July, but..."

"Fireworks, baby." I looked at him, slightly confused. "It's been fireworks since the beginning for us. You want a party, right?" I nodded. "Fourth of July."

"That's only four months away."

"So? Better get to work."

I threw my napkin at him. "You're going to deal with my wrath when I'm pulling my hair out."

"Is that a yes?"

"Ugh." I threw my head back and groaned before conceding. "Yes. You'll lose your independence on Independence Day. How fitting!"

I was laughing as he stalked over and pulled me out of the chair. He pulled the shirt over my head, threw me over his shoulder and smacked my bare ass before dragging me to the shower.

fifteen

~ CALVIN ~

WE WERE GETTING READY TO BOARD the plane home the next day, "Jane, just call Cassidy and ask if they want to have dinner." She was itching to tell somebody about the engagement and she and Cass would want to start their crazy wedding planning immediately.

Smiling, she pulled out her phone and dialed Cass. "Hey Cassidy. Cal and I are getting ready to board our plane. Can you and James meet us for dinner tonight?" She smiled, "Yup, we land shortly after six. How about Antonio's? Ok. We'll see you then."

As she put her phone in her pocket I said, "I'm surprised you didn't tell her."

"I want them to be surprised too! We can tell them tonight."

Once we boarded and got through take-off, I asked her about bridesmaids. "Would you want Becky to be there?"

"I'll invite her, but I kind of had someone else in mind." I wasn't sure who she was referring to and wondered if she was thinking about asking Cassidy. "James has been the one constant in my life. He's my best friend, after you of course."

"So, you want him to be a groomsman?"

"Well, I was thinking he could be *my* best person. He's more than a cousin." She made complete sense even if it was a little untraditional.

I'd thought about asking Paul or Frank to be my Best Man, but wasn't sure whom to pick. It dawned on me who to ask. "I think that's a great idea."

"What about you? Who do you want as your Best Man?"

"I'm going to ask Cassidy. I thought about asking Paul or Frank, but I'm closest with Cassidy. Makes perfect sense."

She clapped like a giddy school girl. "Yay! I'm so excited." Then her face dropped. "Do you think she'll be up to planning *and* being in the wedding?"

"I'm sure she will. Remember, she's a professional!"

We landed several hours later and once we had our luggage, headed to the parking garage. We pulled into Antonio's a little later than we anticipated. I spotted James' truck and parked nearby. Jane had been glowing all day, I had, too. We were so happy and excited to tell our news to everyone.

As soon as Cassidy spotted us, she leapt up to hug us. She seemed happier than the last time I saw her and that eased my worry. She was hugging Jane as James and I exchanged a handshake. It didn't look like I would have to kick his ass after all.

"How was California? Did it go well?" We were grinning like idiots at Cass' question as we took our seats. "What's going on?"

"Go ahead and tell them, baby doll." Smiling, Jane stuck her hand out and showed off her ring.

Cassidy gasped and cried out, jumping out of her seat again. She hugged us both again before taking Jane's hand in hers. James was an idiot as I noticed there was still no ring on my sister's finger. Couldn't he tell by how excited Cass was for Jane that she wanted all the hoopla involved with a wedding?

"I'm so happy!"

James was smiling as the waitress came over. He requested a bottle of champagne for us to celebrate. "Congrats you two. It's about time." He winked as Cass elbowed him causing us all to chuckle.

"So dare I ask when the big day is?" She was always planning ahead.

"Well, you two are the first we've told and we wanted to talk to you first." They nodded as Jane continued. "We'd like you to be our people." The waitress dropped off the champagne and poured us each a glass before stepping away. "Like I was saying, James, I'd like you to be my Best Man."

James seemed confused at Jane's words. "Don't you mean Calvin's Best Man?"

I interjected, "No, she was correct. I'd like Cassidy to be my Maid of Honor."

"Matron, she's married." Jane corrected me as I rolled my eyes and she said, "I want James standing by me and Calvin wants Cassidy with him."

"There's really no other option. If you say no, then the wedding's off." Cassidy caught my sarcastic tone and smiled.

"Yes! Of course. I'm in. What do you say, James?"

His expression was somber as we waited for his answer. "You had me at 'We'd like you to be our people.'" He smiled as Jane released a pleased breath, "Of course. It would be an honor. But like Cassidy asked. Have you set a date? I'll mark off a few hours to get you to the church on time." His sarcasm was laced with good will.

"You tell them. It was your idea."

I spilled the news and the date. "So, it's been fireworks since the beginning for the two of us. In keeping with tradition, we want fireworks at the wedding too. July fourth."

"Of this year?" Cassidy grew pale at the thought and I wanted to bust up laughing. "Please tell me its next year."

"Nope. This year. And we want you to plan it!" Cassidy looked panicked. "I'll pay whatever fees are required. Well, mom and dad will! And we were hoping The Benedict ballroom was available."

James pulled out his phone. "Hold please. Checking now." He called someone and asked the question. "Great. I need you to book it now for the Whitford-Charles wedding. Thank you. Okay, talk to you soon." Putting his phone back in his pocket, "It's all yours."

Jane clapped like a giddy schoolgirl, which I hoped didn't become a habit. Who was I kidding? It was endearing. Cassidy was still speechless.

"Cassidy, are you alright?" She was going to make me pay for this.

"Me? Yes, just a lot to do. We'll have to get started with the planning right away. Are you free on Monday, Jane?"

"Yup. I can stop in after my shift if you like."

"Great. I'll pull Lena in on this too. We'll have to double team it to get it done."

"Anything you need, just let me or my mom know. You know she's going to want to be involved with all the planning." I wrapped my arm around her shoulder as her and Cassidy prattled on.

When we left the restaurant, Jane insisted that we swing by her parent's house to tell them the news. I figured it was too late in the day, but she was right. When we got there her parents were still up. Her father greeted us and he seemed a little concerned at our late night visit.

"Have you spoken to your mother?" Her dad was visibly shaken as Jane assured him everything was fine.

"Daddy, what's wrong?"

"Your mother is over at your Uncle's house."

A shadow fell over Jane's face. "No." She fumbled in her purse and like she knew it was coming it began ringing. She answered it, "Mom, what's going on?"

She stepped away as her dad filled me in. Eva had taken a sudden turn for the worse a couple hours prior. He was waiting on a call from Bev to see how grave it was. Jane ended the call and came over.

"She said it's bad. It'll probably happen soon." I pulled her close as she started crying. "I have to go over there."

"Of course." Her dad rode with us as we headed over to say our goodbyes to Eva.

Bev greeted us when we got there and we walked to the living room. Jane and her sat down on the couch and consoled each other. Beverly took Jane's hand in hers and noticed the ring.

"What's this?"

Jane smiled through the tears and croaked out, "I said yes."

Jane and her mother were like a couple of school girls as their squeals pierced my ears through their tears. I was bombarded with a hug from her mom as she congratulated us. "When's the big day?"

"Fourth of July!"

Her dad smiled as her mom asked, "Of next year right?" Jane just shook her head. "Good grief Jane. Are you trying to kill me?" Jane's eyes bulged out, given the circumstances. "Sorry, bad choice of words."

"It's ok. Besides, you have plenty of time to help and I'll need it. James secured the ballroom and I'm meeting with Cassidy on Monday to start planning. Well, I think I am. Now with this. I don't know what will happen." Jane started crying again. "I want her at my wedding."

"Oh, Janey. She wants to be there, too. Let's just see what happens."

J.J. walked over then, having overheard the end of their conversation.

He looked worse for wear, but smiled at us. "What a whirlwind. I'm so happy for you two. Things are looking up for you both."

"Yes, they are. I expect my first grandchild by next fall." Nothing like pressure. Bev winked at us both as Jane chastised her. I wanted kids, but a little time alone with my wife would be nice too.

J.J. offered up one of the guest rooms and we accepted. We had a suitcase full of clothes in Jane's car. I had just finished carrying our bags to our room and was looking for Cassidy, when I spotted her walking out the patio door. She was crying and I wondered if Eva had passed.

Walking up behind her, I put my hand on her shoulder, not wanting to startle her. She turned and the flood gates opened when she saw me. I pulled her to me and tried to console her.

"H, he, won't survive this Cal. It's going to k, kill him."

"It's okay. He'll get through it with you beside him." I stroked her hair, trying anything to calm her down.

"I hope you're right."

"It won't be easy. Jane has said the same things." Jane knew how hard it would be on James and had voiced her concerns to me.

Pulling away she asked, "Is she here?"

"Yes, she's saying her goodbyes. You coming back in?"

"Not yet. Go find Jane. I'll be okay." I hugged her again before walking inside in search of Jane.

sixteen

~ JANE ~

I WAS WANDERING THE HALLS OF THE house that had been a second home to me growing up. I had spent so many days, nights, and holidays there as a child. Aunt Eva loved Christmas and always had a huge celebration, when she was still healthy. She'd been battling that cursed cancer for far too long. I told myself that it would be a relief knowing she wasn't in pain any more. But I would miss her terribly.

Making my way to her room, I stepped in and took in my surroundings. James was sitting by her bedside and appeared to be sleeping. Eva was also sleeping. This all seemed so wrong. I had just seen James a couple hours ago and we had been laughing and having a good time and planning my wedding.

Walking over to him, I touched his shoulder and he lifted his head to me. His eyes were puffy and he was holding on by a thread. Bending down so I could wrap my arms around him, he returned the gesture.

"I'm so sorry, James. Is there anything I can do?" He just shook his head.

"Jane, is that you?" We both turned to look at the sound of her voice. James stood and gave me his seat next to her and I watched as he moved to the foot of the bed. "How was California?"

I couldn't help, but smile. "Oh, it was fine. Actually, it was really good. We're getting married, Aunt Eva."

A smile spread across my Aunt's beautiful face as I showed her my ring. "I'm so happy. He'll always protect you. He loves you so much. Your life is waiting for you and he'll be a great partner."

"I know. He's amazing. I'm blessed." Though I tried to fight it, I started crying.

"It's okay, Janey. I won't be far away."

"I'm just going to miss you so much."

"Me too. But someone needs to keep Jason company. He's been alone too long."

Thinking about her being gone along with Jason had me nearly convulsing. Standing up, I reached down and hugged her. I noticed James wiping at his own tears.

I tried to lighten the mood, "Do you remember that time when Jason trapped me up in the treehouse? I wouldn't leave you two alone and he tricked me into going up there and then took the ladder down."

We all laughed at that. I was furious for days after that happened. I was scared to death and too little to climb down the tree by myself. Aunt Eva had eventually heard me crying and dragged Jason by his ear through the yard. That itself made everything all better. Soon she fell asleep and I got up to leave the room.

"James. You're going to make it." He didn't say anything, but walked me to the door. I hugged him and then went in search of Cassidy. She was who he needed, not me.

When I found her, she was asleep on the couch. I debated whether or not I should wake her, but went ahead and did so. Eva had asked to see Cassidy before she fell asleep and I assumed James would be there too. "She's asking for you."

"Oh, okay." Cassidy got up and headed toward Aunt Eva's room.

I went to the guest room and crawled into bed next to Cal. I didn't have to ask for him to hold me, he did it without asking.

"I love you, Cal."

"I love you too, baby doll."

When I woke, I looked to the clock and realized I'd only slept for a few hours. I got up and went to check for an update. I found mom in the kitchen and she confirmed that Eva was still holding on, but they didn't expect it to be much longer.

"Jane, there's nothing more you can do here. Why don't you go home?"

"I can't go home."

"Yes, you can dear. Eva wouldn't want you here worrying for her. I'll call you every couple hours." She hugged me and kissed my head. "Jane, you've been traveling all week. Go home and get some rest."

I just nodded and headed back to the guest room. Cal was up and getting dressed. "I think I want to go home."

"Jane? Is she…"

"No, not yet. But, I said goodbye. I just want to go home."

"Ok. Whatever you want."

We were headed out when he spotted Cassidy. "I'll be right back."

Cal and Cassidy talked for a couple minutes, but I didn't see James anywhere. Cassidy headed toward the kitchen as Cal and I left. "She ok?"

"She will be. She asked if I could swing by her place and feed the cat." I tried not to be annoyed, but he caught my expression. "I can take you home first, that was my plan anyways."

"Sorry. Ok. I just want to crawl into our bed."

Cal walked me in and made sure everything was ok. Always the cop. I didn't bother going through the mail that Cassidy had stacked on the counter for us. Instead, once Cal gave the all clear, I marched upstairs and stripped off my clothes and climbed into bed.

He kissed my temple, "I'll be back soon. Get some rest."

I think I fell asleep before he even left the room.

~ CALVIN ~

I GOT IN MY truck and headed toward Cassidy's place. The new Goo Goo Dolls album was in the CD player and I put it to *BulletProofAngel*. The lyrics reminded me of something Eva had said to me the night before.

After speaking with Cassidy on the patio, I'd gone in search of Jane. Not being able to find her, I headed toward Eva's bedroom thinking I'd find Jane there. Quietly, I walked in and didn't see Jane. Only J.J. and Eva occupied the room.

"Calvin, please come in." I thought she had been asleep, but she wasn't.

Walking closer to her bed she insisted I sit down. "I don't want to bother you."

"Stop it. I hear you're joining the family. I'd like to get to know you a little better since my time is ending." I was surprised at her candor and J.J. just smiled.

I sat down in the chair and asked, "What do you want to know?"

"Tell me everything." I laughed at that. "How are you doing? Apparently you're bulletproof."

"I wouldn't say bulletproof, but I'm good. It wasn't my time." I immediately regretted my words and she picked up on my discomfort.

"It's ok. My time's been coming for quite a while. And now, clearly it wasn't your time. She's a lot different than your sister, but I've watched a small change in her, since you came around." I tilted my head at her, not sure of her meaning. "Cassidy wears her heart on her sleeve and isn't afraid to express her emotions. She thinks it's a weakness, your sister that is. It's not.

"Jane envies that in your sister. She was very tenderhearted as a child. But that changed when we lost Jason. I don't think I've seen Jane shed a tear in almost ten years, not until you came into her life. You've broken down walls that we all thought were indestructible."

I was flattered and not sure what to say. "Thank you, Mrs. Benedict."

"Please, call me Eva."

"Eva. Jane and James seem to be a lot alike. Cassidy and I have never shied away from our emotions."

"Yes, you're right. Losing Jason changed both of them and not for the better. How could it not?" She yawned and I thought she'd dozed off when I went to stand. She reached for my hand and I was started by how cold it was. "Take care of her. And don't be afraid to put James in his place if he gets out of line with your sister. But remember he loves her."

Smirking, I said, "I will." I leaned down and kissed her cheek. "It was a pleasure getting to know you. I'm sorry we didn't have more time together."

"In another life." She winked and I nodded to J.J. and left the room.

I remembered her calling me bulletproof and replayed the song. She was an incredible lady and I was sad about not getting to know her better. It made me miss my own mother. I was angry about the lost years with her and probably always would be. Though it was different, I couldn't imagine the pain James was experiencing. He was very protective, an only child, and he was very close to his mom. Jane and Cass had every reason to worry that Eva's death would destroy him. Losing my mother had almost destroyed me.

I got to Cassidy's place and fed the cat. Everything seemed to be in place. I emptied her mailbox and put it on her counter before heading out. When I got back home, Jane was sound asleep. I decided to get a workout in and headed to the spare room and hit the weight bench.

The next morning, we got the phone call we were dreading. Eva was gone. Jane and I sat on the couch for a while as I held her. Her phone rang again, it was her mom.

"Hey. Ok. No, I can do whatever's needed. I'm not working those days, but I work tonight. Ok. Love you, too."

"Jane, you should try to get some rest." I forgot she had to work that night.

"I know. I have that meeting with Cassidy in the morning, too, if she's at work."

"Is there anything I can do?"

"No, you're doing it."

seventeen

~ JANE ~

I MADE IT TO WORK THAT NIGHT AFTER A short, but well-needed nap. It was my first night back on the regular rotation and I was happy for the distraction. Everyone seemed welcoming and if they were wondering if I had gotten away with murder, I was none the wiser. We weren't slammed, but had just enough deliveries to keep a steady pace all night long.

By the time I got home from work, Cal had already left for work. I changed my clothes, brewed some coffee, and scanned my emails before heading over to Cassidy's office. I wasn't even sure if she'd be in or not, but was hoping she would be. I figured we could both use the distraction.

I made it up to her floor and the receptionist let me back. I knocked on her open door and she jumped slightly. She looked exhausted. Her hair was pulled up and she was wearing her glasses, which she didn't often wear.

She looked surprised to see me as I asked, "Hey, do you still have time to meet?"

"Yes, of course." Cassidy stood and motioned me into the room and I took the empty seat across from her. "Are you up to it? I wasn't sure if you'd make it in today or not."

"Same to you. I wasn't sure you'd be here either." I sat down and noticed that her eyes were puffy and had to ask, "How is he?" She didn't respond, but the expression on her face told me everything I suspected and needed to know. "That bad, huh."

"Yeah, I'd say so." She sat down and pulled a notepad out of her desk. "Is it okay if we talk about the wedding? I don't want to be pushy."

It was bad. She didn't even want to talk about him or Eva. I understood that. "Yes, of course. Eva would want me to press on."

"Okay, so on the Fourth of July, at The Benedict. Are there any other bridesmaids?"

"Nope, just you and James." I momentarily pictured James in a bridesmaid dress and inwardly laughed.

"Colors? We should send out your invitations pronto. Do you want a bridal shower?"

"The bridal shower isn't necessary, but definitely want a bachelorette party!" That got a laugh out of her. "And green. Some shade of green. I know I should go with navy or red, but I want green."

"It's your wedding. Let me go grab the book of invitations from Lena. I'll be right back." The second she stood up, Lena walked in the room like she knew she was needed. "Perfect. It's like you read my mind."

Lena sat down in the empty chair next to me as I looked through the binder full of invitations. I was torn between two and Cassidy seemed to read my mind.

"He won't care which one you pick. Get the one *you* like." I laughed and pointed to the one on my right. "Perfect." Cassidy put the book on the credenza behind her and grabbed another. "Flowers. Any thoughts?"

"Um, no. Flowers aren't my thing. Meaning, I know what a rose is and that's about it."

Lena started showing us some of her thoughts, given my color choices, the time of year, and location. I told them I didn't want anything too over the top. It just wasn't me. Cassidy promised she wouldn't go overboard and would take care of it. I picked out some flowers I liked that Cassidy and Lena suggested.

Cal and I wanted to get married outside, weather permitting, because the courtyard was so beautiful. We had yet to see it in the summertime, but loved it in winter so we weren't too concerned. It was going to be beautiful, Cassidy would make sure of it. By the time we finished up, I was exhausted. We'd worked up through lunch and I knew if I was going to make it to work that night, I had to get home and get some rest.

"Okay. I have to go. I'm exhausted." She nodded her ok as it dawned on me that I needed to start looking for a dress. "Would you be willing to go dress shopping with me next week?" The upcoming week would just be impossible with all the funeral arrangements.

"Sure. I'd love that!" She walked me to the door and hugged me before I headed home.

I struggled to stay awake on the way home, but was thankful it was a short drive. Stripping down into my underwear and a tank, I crawled into bed once I set my alarm.

WE WERE STANDING in the cemetery and the burial service was almost over. It was a chilly day and expected to snow at any time. The whole week had been a blur. Cal had been wonderful and very attentive, like he always was. I was off work until Sunday night and looking forward to visiting with family after the burial.

The next Wednesday, Cassidy and I met for lunch before heading out for a day of dress shopping. I was excited and nervous all at the same time. I'd never tried on a wedding dress before. I had dresses in my closet, but hated picking them out. I was more comfortable in my scrubs or jeans and a t-shirt.

"Is your mom coming?"

"She's going to meet us at the bridal salon. She had a lunch appointment of her own." Cassidy nodded as we looked over the menu. "So, how are things?"

She stared at the menu for a moment before looking at me. "Don't ask." She was angry. I'd heard about her temper, but never experienced it firsthand. I reached my hand out and squeezed hers. "Cassidy, you can trust me. I know he can be a royal pain in the ass."

Sighing, she told me about the concussion he had sustained before the funeral. She also told me that he had packed some things and was staying at the hotel and that she hadn't seen or spoken to him since the night of the funeral. I didn't know what to say. It was understandable that he was grieving and we all knew—and warned Cassidy—that he would push her away. But for him to be staying at the hotel royally pissed me off.

"Cass, I can talk to him if you want." She shook her head vehemently. "Give him some time. He's horribly independent. He'll come around. He just needs some space to process everything. He'll be back."

She just shrugged her shoulders. "I know." I wasn't used to this side of her. She was trying to brush it off like it was no big deal. They were married. It was a HUGE deal. She looked to me and said, "Please don't tell Cal. He'll go off the deep end." I agreed with her, but wasn't sure how long we would be able to keep it from him, if James didn't get his act together.

We made it to the salon and mom walked in a few minutes later. The sales attendant that I had my appointment, with was very nice. She asked what I liked and didn't like, but I really wasn't sure. I looked to Cassidy and asked her if she had any thoughts.

"Well, it's a Fourth of July wedding, outside in the early evening." She looked at me and seemed to be thinking. "Trumpet, mermaid or traditional A-line would probably be the most flattering. You don't seem like the ball gown type. Strapless, maybe."

My eyes got big at that, "I don't have boobs big enough to hold up a strapless dress!"

We all shared a laugh. "Honey, we can fix that." The sales lady then asked my mom, "Is there anything you'd like to see her in?"

"I'll be happy to see her in a dress. It's like pulling teeth with this one." I rolled my eyes at her. "A train would be nice, maybe a puddle train, and a veil of some sort."

"Ugh. That shit in your face is beautiful, but so annoying mom." My filter had left me for a moment as Cassidy busted up laughing. "And no lace. I'm not an antique table to put a doily on."

"Ok. No lace and no veil, at least not covering her face. What about just a veil in back?"

Mom and I both agreed that might work.

"Ok. I'm going to go grab some dresses. Feel free to pull a few off the rack if they catch your eye."

I walked around with Cassidy and my mom as we looked at dresses. I really didn't know what I wanted. I just knew that I wanted to feel sexy and beautiful. I wanted to see Cal's jaw hit the floor. After we had four to five dresses picked out, I headed to the dressing room while Cassidy and mom waited in the small attached viewing area. We had our own small area, safe from any prying eyes.

Agreeing to show them all the dresses I tried on, I stepped out of the room in the first dress and they sent me right back in. A few dresses later, I was getting discouraged. There was a knock on the door. I opened it up and Cassidy came in, the attendant stepped out to give us some privacy.

"You ok?"

"It's silly. It's just a dress. Why can't I pick one?"

"Cuz it's THEE dress." I heaved a big breath as she smiled at me. "I know you mentioned no lace, that it was too vintage, but will you try on a couple?"

"Sure. Couldn't hurt."

"Yay! Ok. Give me a couple minutes."

Several minutes later, the attendant walked in with three dresses that were covered in lace. The first one was too modest and covered every inch of me except my arms. The next one I actually liked and so did Cassidy and mom.

"We're getting closer. Try on the third one." I rolled my eyes at Cassidy, but agreed.

I put the third one on and was self-conscious because it was nearly backless. It fit well and I was eager to see it the mirror, since there wasn't one in the dressing room. When I walked out, Cassidy and my mom were both speechless.

"What's wrong?"

"Oh, Janey."

"Look in the mirror." Cassidy stood up as I climbed the pedestal and looked in the mirror.

I couldn't speak. The dress was form fitting through the hips where it spilled down my legs and had a puddle train. The top wasn't too revealing, but the back made up for that. Turning to look at the back, I became a basket of nerves.

"Is it too revealing? The back I mean." I looked to my mom and she just shook her head. She was no help at all. "Cass?"

"Jane, it's stunning on you. I think it's just the right amount of elegant and sexy. Here."

She pulled the hair clip out of her hair and twisted mine up so it was off my back. The sales girl helped her and they put a modest tiara on my head which I shook my head at. Then they tried a long, sheer veil on the back and my mom started crying. I looked in the mirror again.

"Can we change the satin sash and bow to green, to match my colors?"

"Absolutely."

I looked myself over again before I said, "I think this is it."

Mom paid for the dress and we made an appointment to come back in a few weeks for my first fitting and to look for a dress for Cassidy.

"Thank you so much for all your help today."

"Please. I'm so happy to call you my sister. I always wanted one."

"Feeling is mutual. Call me if you need to vent. Don't worry about James. He loves you."

I INVITED CASSIDY to the concert the following weekend and she had agreed. When I told her that Cal had invited Paul, she seemed a little surprised.

"James won't mind and I don't have anyone else to ask."

"James will get over it if he does. Besides, he doesn't like country music." We both laughed at her statement knowing it was true. He wouldn't be caught dead at a country music concert.

eighteen

WE WERE GETTING READY FOR THE concert and waiting for
Paul and Cassidy to pick us up. I'd voiced my concern to Jane
and she assured me that everything was fine. James didn't like country
music and was fine with Cassidy going with us.

I pulled my boots on as Jane walked out of the closet. She was
wearing jeans, that looked painted on, and a red top that exposed her
midriff slightly. She was wearing cowboy boots, too.

"Nope, go put on a something else. You're not leaving the house
looking like that."

"Looking like what!"

"Dangerous and…" I watched as she put on a cowboy hat and my
cock twitched. "Shit. Good enough to eat."

She winked at me, "I *am* good enough to eat!" I stalked over to her
and she handed me my shirt. "Not now, Officer Charles. We have to

be ready when they get here!" I groaned my disapproval. "Hey, you're the one who wanted to get there early so we could tailgate."

"Yeah, yeah." I put on my black shirt, leaving several buttons undone and put on my hat.

She whistled at me as we heard the horn of Paul's SUV. "Let's go, hot stuff!"

Jane and I climbed in the backseat as we headed to the show. "Come on man. Put on some country!"

Everyone laughed as Cassidy took control of the radio and surfed the channels. When we pulled into the parking lot at the venue, we were all signing along to *This Is How We Roll* by Florida Georgia Line. We were all in a great mood and enjoyed a drink before heading inside.

Jane floored us all as we were headed to our seats. She pulled VIP passes out of her purse. I wasn't sure what it meant, but I was stoked. We were escorted to side stage and enjoyed some drinks and appetizers as the band members set up the stage.

"Jane, this is awesome!"

"I know. I rock!"

Kip Moore walked right by us, nodded his head and smiled. He stopped a few feet in front of us and once the lights went down, he headed out on to the stage and took his place. He started playing the guitar rift for one of his recent hits, though the band extended it out while the crowd started cheering. *Dirt Road* filled the auditorium as the four of us stood no more than fifteen feet away. Kip started singing as we watched.

I took Jane's hand as we moved to the beat. Cassidy and Paul were next to us, just bouncing to the beat of the music. The crowd went crazy a few songs later when they broke into *Somethin' 'Bout A Truck* and then *Beer Money*. The four of us danced as Paul and I twirled Cassidy and Jane around the side of the stage.

Pulling Jane to my front, she leaned back against me while we enjoyed the rest of the show. I felt like he was there performing for only us. The show was nearing the end when he introduced his newest single *Young Love*. When the song was over, the lights went down and Kip walked off stage. He stood right by us and gathered with his band as the crowd went crazy. There was only one more song I wanted to hear and hoped it was part of his encore.

They headed back on stage and broke into *Hey Pretty Girl*. Jane and I were slow dancing when I spotted Paul's arms around Cassidy's shoulders. It infuriated me. She was married and they were crossing a line. At least I felt that they were.

"Cal, they're just friends."

I brought my attention back to Jane and sighed. "Something's off. Do you know anything?"

"I know Cass and James were having a hard time right after the funeral, but Cassidy told me last week that everything was fine." She kissed my cheek as I tried to focus on her and the rest of the song.

We got to meet Kip and the band after the show. He was a cool guy, but we didn't stay too long. He signed the shirts and CDs we purchased and we made our way out to the parking lot. Jane and Cass were walking together and I slowed down so that I could chat with Paul. He needed a reminder that my baby sister was off limits.

"What are you doing?"

He looked to me, clueless. I motioned my head toward Cassidy and he said, "Nothing. We're friends."

"Looked like you wanted more than friendship back there." I was trying to keep my voice down, so that Cass and Jane didn't get involved.

He shook his head and was becoming agitated. "Everything isn't what it seems."

Jane and Cassidy looked back to us just as I spit out, "She's married. You need to back off."

The four of us were standing in close quarters when Paul raked his hands over his face and yelled, "Well maybe someone should remind James of that." What the fuck was he talking about? "I'm sorry, Cassidy, but they need to know how he's treating you."

Cassidy looked to me and I could see the shame and embarrassment on her face. What the hell had happened? Instead of saying anything she turned toward Paul's SUV and walked away.

"Cass, wait." Paul and Jane stayed back as I caught up to Cassidy. When I knew we were a safe distance away I asked her, "What's going on? Did something happen?"

"That's just it. Nothing's happened. I haven't seen him since Eva's funeral. And the day she died he moved out, I think."

WHAT! The funeral was weeks ago. "What?" I was enraged.

"I'll handle it, Cal. I need to confront him and I will."

Confront him? He needed his ass kicked. "I'll kill him."

Jane walked up on us, concern in her voice. "Kill who?"

"Your fucking cousin has walked out on my sister!" I knew it wasn't Jane's fault, but I was pissed.

"What are you talking about? Cassidy, why didn't you tell me?"

If Jane knew what was going on and hadn't told me...FUCK. I couldn't take it anymore. "Let's go. When I get my hands on him."

Paul dropped Cassidy off first and I walked her to her door. Hugging her I told her, "He's going to make this right. I'll make sure of it. You know you can come stay with Jane and me if you don't want to be alone. You can bring the cat."

She let out a sad attempt at a laugh and responded, "Um, no thanks. I don't need you two reminding me at every turn what I've lost."

"Cass..."

"Go. Your fiancé is waiting for you."

I climbed in to the front seat and turned to look at Paul and Jane.

"Someone better tell me what the fuck is going on, right now!"

Paul pulled away from Cassidy's and made the five minute drive to my place. "All I know is that he's hurt her terribly. And she's made it clear to me that she's still in love with him. Maybe Jane knows something more than that. I'm just trying to be a friend."

"What the fuck ever? You don't know how to be *friends* with a woman."

"Screw you, Calvin."

"HEY! Knock it off, you two." Jane shouted over both of us as Paul pulled in the driveway. "Paul isn't the problem here. James is."

"You can say that again." I turned to Jane wanting more info. "What do you know?"

"Guys, I don't want to hear any more. He's my boss, she's my… friend. It's complicated enough."

"Alright man. I'm sorry. I'm trusting you to be a good *friend* to her." He nodded as I got out of the vehicle and Jane did the same. He pulled away before we were even inside.

"You're being too hard on him."

"Be careful Jane. I'm going to take it out on your cousin."

"He's going through a lot."

"Fuck that bullshit. He's acting like a douchebag." She walked in the front door and headed up the stairs. "Jane, I'm sorry." I knew she was stuck between a rock and a hard place. I followed her up to the bedroom and she was already getting undressed.

"I don't want to talk about my cousin and your sister. I want to enjoy the rest of our night." Smiling I walked a little closer as she dangled handcuffs between us. "I'm ready for my strip search, Officer Charles. I've been very bad."

nineteen

~ JANE ~

I TRIED REACHING OUT TO JAMES, but he wouldn't return my calls or texts. I was going to have to surprise him at work one day. Heading over to pick up Cassidy, I had my first fitting and we were going to pick her dress as well.

Pulling in her driveway, there was no sign of James. A feeling of dread settled over me, but I wasn't sure why or what it was. Walking to the front door, I knocked and waited.

When I heard the knob turning, I plastered a big smile on my face. I was looking forward to some girl time, just her and I. She looked like she'd been run over by a Mack truck. "You look like shit. Were you sleeping?"

"Thanks. Just a short nap." I analyzed her, knowing more was going on as she stated plainly, "I haven't heard from him."

"What the hell is wrong with him?" It'd been WEEKS. Cass

just shook her head as I tried to apologize for my cousin. "I'm sorry Cassidy. I knew he'd take his mom's death hard, but I didn't expect him to shut you out."

"I just don't know what to do. We're married, yet I have no husband." Putting on her jacket and grabbing her purse she went on, "I've tried talking to him, but nothing works."

"I'm going to talk to him." We got in my car and drove away.

"No, really it's okay."

"It's not okay. If your brother catches wind of how bad this really is, James is going to regret it."

"Yea, him and Paul both." Paul? What did that mean? I thought they were just friends. "There's nothing going on between Paul and me."

"You sure about that?" Maybe Cal was right about them.

Sighing, "He was my first love, we have history. What am I supposed to say? He's been a perfect gentleman and a good friend. There's nothing else to discuss."

I believed her. She was too upset about James for me to doubt her. Though I knew deep down that Paul wanted more from her. "Okay. Sorry, it's just…"

"What, Jane? Just say it."

She didn't know, but it was written all over the walls. "You know he's in love with you, right?"

"James?"

"No, Paul!" Why were people so dense about what was going on around them? I was guilty of it too.

"What are you talking about?"

"Cassidy, don't play dumb. Paul is head over heels for you. And if my cousin isn't careful, Paul's going to snatch you away." It would serve James right.

My first fitting went as planned and we found a beautiful green dress for Cassidy. She was breathtaking in the dress and it complimented all that red hair of hers. I had picked out a few that I preferred and let her decide on the one she liked most. James would swoon when he saw her in it. Paul would, too. I sighed, anticipating how messy things were about to get with the three of them.

After I dropped her off, I called James and got voicemail again. Cal and I crawled into bed that night chatting about wedding plans.

"How's Cassidy?"

"Good." I hated lying to him, but I wanted to give James a chance to explain himself before I threw him under the bus.

The next morning, I tried calling James again. "Jackson James Benedict the third. If you don't call me back, you're going to regret it. Cassidy is a wreck. We NEED to talk." I disconnected the call and set my cell on the counter.

"Jane?"

I jumped and turned to find Cal standing nearby. He must've gotten up and I hadn't heard him. Shit. "Cal…"

"She's not ok, is she?"

I just shook my head as he went back up the stairs. I followed after him, but he wouldn't listen. He got dressed and walked out the door. I wasn't sure if he was headed toward James or Cassidy. I knew that keeping it from him had been a mistake. I felt terrible and prayed he'd be forgiving and understand why I hadn't told him right away.

~ CALVIN ~

I PULLED IN HER drive and spotted Paul's vehicle and saw red. Throwing my truck in park, I ran up her steps and pounded on the door as I pulled out my key. Walking in, I saw Paul and shoved him as hard as I could. "She's married. I told you to stay away from her."

He didn't stumble back far, yelling back, "And I told you, maybe somebody should remind James of that. Look at her."

My eyes darted to my sister and she looked horrible. Had she been sleeping? Had she caught him cheating, or him her? I didn't know what to think. "Cassidy, what's going on?"

"He, I, it's complicated."

Paul was pacing a path in the floor. "Isn't it obvious? He's left her."

"What?" I tilted her chin so she would look at me. "Cassidy, what happened?"

"It's complicated."

I walked back over to Paul and he told me that James had moved out. He'd left her high and dry. "Where is he?"

"At the office, would be my guess. He's been sleeping there and I'm supposed to be there soon for a meeting."

"Cal, please let it go."

"I will not." Let it go? Not until I got my hands on him. I walked toward the door.

Cassidy cried out, "What are you going to do?"

"I'm going to UN-complicate it." Slamming the door I got in my truck and headed to his office building. Security didn't want to let me up, but the minute I showed my badge they waved me through. I ran into Smith, who was surprised to see me, but knew without question why I was there.

"You need to calm down. There are things going on. We're doubling the guards on Cassidy and Melissa. Dan is behind more than we thought he was."

"Jesus Christ. Smith, I can't talk about this now. I need to see him, NOW."

Smith stepped out from in front of the conference room, the same room we'd met in several times over the past couple of months. Smith followed in behind me as I found James standing over some blueprints.

"You mind telling me what the fuck is going on with you and my sister?"

He looked back to the blueprints and murmured, "Hello, Calvin."

Pompous ass. "I just left from seeing her and she was a puddle on the floor, crying on Paul's shoulder. What did you do?"

"Cal, what happens between my wife and me is our business."

"See, that's where I'm confused. A *husband* wouldn't let his wife cry on the shoulder of another man." I walked over to his side of the table getting nose to nose with him and spewed, "You fucking make this right with her or end it now. She deserves at least that for all she's put up with and done for you."

He had almost half a smirk on his face as he casually said, "She's already moved on. I don't know what more she could want from me."

Dead. I was going to kill him. My fist reared back as I clocked him in the face. He stumbled back and I delivered another blow to his gut as he fell to the ground. He wasn't putting up a fight and I was glad. Blow after blow, I bloodied his pretty-boy face and then felt myself being pulled off of him. I didn't fight it. I'd sent my message to him, loud and clear.

Rubbing my knuckles, I chimed, "You're a piece of shit, Benedict." I walked out the door and passed by Paul, who I assume saw it all. "That's what happens when you fuck with my sister. You've been warned." Paul didn't say anything and I headed to the elevator.

I walked in the door back home and Jane kept her distance from me. She was right to do so. I didn't want to lash out at her and I knew she couldn't control what happened between James and Cassidy. We were having dinner at her parents' house that night so I had to get myself under control by then.

"I'm going to the gym. I'll be back in time to go to dinner."

"Ok."

I kissed her cheek and said, "I love you. I just need to blow off some steam."

"Ok. Love you, too."

I WAS IN THE closet looking for something to wear when Jane wrapped her arms around me. She rested her head on my back and whispered, "I'm sorry."

Turning, I said, "It's not your fault. I just can't watch her get hurt. She's been through so much, especially in the past year."

She took my hands in hers, "Your hands are bruised." She looked to my face, "Cal?"

"James may have fallen into my fist." Her eyes got big, "He'll be alright."

"You men. Not every problem can be solved with your fists."

"Maybe not, but it sure felt good."

Rolling her eyes she said, "I'll be downstairs. Hurry up."

Dinner was fine until J.J. started complaining of chest pain. Jane immediately took over and asked him questions. He had joined us for dinner and I couldn't help, but feel guilty knowing I'd given his son a beating earlier in the day. Jane insisted on calling an ambulance and rode with him to the hospital.

After a couple hours at the hospital we were headed home. J.J. had a heart attack, but was expected to make a full recovery. Jane was beat as we walked in the door. I knew she was upset, too, because James wasn't answering his phone.

"I should call Cassidy and let her know."

"In the morning. He's going to be fine. It can wait."

Jane was still asleep in the morning so I decided to call Cassidy and let her know what was going on with J.J. She said she was headed up there and asked that I meet her there. That was fine with me. I hopped in the shower and was examining my bruised knuckles, when I heard the shower curtain slide open.

Jane stepped into the shower with me and just stared at me as her hands ran over my torso. Her hand trailed down my thigh and back up to stroke me. My cock immediately responded to her as I murmured her name.

"Shh. I don't want to talk."

Groaning, I leaned down and kissed her. Her velvet tongue glided over mine as I pushed her up against the shower wall. She protested as the cold tiles pressed against her back. I reached down and pulled her legs around my waist. She started to speak and I stopped her.

"No talking."

Her eyes were still glazed over from sleep, when I entered her. We both gasped out as her walls gripped me like a vice. She rocked her hips back and I slammed into her. Her arms wrapped around my shoulders and my lips grazed her collar bone.

"Cal, fuck me."

I swore my cock grew an inch at her words. Losing all thought of her pleasure, I sought my own as I thrust in and out of her. I needed the release and she encouraged me on.

"Do it, fuck me till you come." I let out a guttural moan when my cock unleashed its load inside her. Panting against her neck, I realized my blunder. "Feel better?"

"Yes and no. Now it's your turn." I reached for the shower head and pulled it off the wall. "I've heard women enjoy this."

She smirked and denied it saying, "I don't' know what you're talking about."

"I think you do, baby doll."

I brought the shower head closer as the water sprayed over her. Closing her eyes, she moaned as I let the water get closer. Lifting one foot, she placed it on the soap holder to give me better access. Her hands gripped my forearms as she pulled me to her.

"Don't be jealous of how quick it'll happen." She was breathless, whispering against my chest.

"Not jealous. Enthralled!"

"Oh, right there."

"Look at me baby. I want to watch you come." Reaching from behind, with my free hand, I slid two fingers into her and began sliding them in and out, careful to let the water continue spraying over her clit.

"Cal!"

Her eyes met mine and I watched her pupils change as she cried out. She was trembling in my arms as her orgasm claimed her. Dropping the shower head, I rubbed her clit until she begged me to stop. I held her to me until she could stand on her own.

"You ok?"

"Mmm. I'm perfect."

"Good. I have to go. You going to be ok?" She looked to me and I told her, "I'm meeting Cassidy at the hospital. Do you want to come?"

"No. You go ahead. I'll visit with him before work."

"Love you."

"I know." She smacked my ass as I climbed out of the shower.

twenty

~ CALVIN ~

I WAS MAKING THE TWENTY minute drive to the hospital when I got a call from Smith. Cassidy had been attacked outside the hospital, suspicions were pointing to Dan. Smith assured me that she was ok. I floored it and when I got there, a flurry of police cars were around the West entrance. I flashed my badge at the valet and ran over.

Cassidy was sitting on a bench, with Paul beside her. Smith found me and gave me a few more details. Apparently he and Paul were headed into the hospital when they spotted Cassidy leaving. A car flew up next to her and someone jumped out of the passenger side and made a grab for her. Smith said he and Paul started running toward her, but that she was putting up one hell of a fight.

"Did you teach her that?"

"Teach her what?"

"You would've been proud. She obliterated the guy with classic defense moves."

I laughed at that. "Thank fucking God I showed her!"

"You can say that again."

"What were you guys doing here, anyway?"

"We dropped off James and were walking back from parking the car when it all happened."

"So where the fuck is James. Why isn't he here with her?"

"Really, dude? I think your beating yesterday was warning enough." He patted my arm. "It's all good. Did it feel good? I've wanted to beat his ass for weeks, but I need my job."

I laughed at that. "Yes. It felt damn good."

"In all seriousness, he doesn't know what happened. She wouldn't let us call him."

I nodded and made my way over to Cassidy and Paul vacated his seat for me. She looked up at me and I hugged her to me. "Thank God, you're ok. Did he hurt you?"

"No, I think I'm ok." She looked to the patrol car that the guy was sitting in and I sensed something was going on in that brain of hers. "Cass, what is it?"

"Cal, I need to see him."

"That's not a great idea."

"Cal, I think he's the same guy who tried attacking me at the office. I need to see his eyes."

Shit. This was good and bad. If it was him, why was he so hell-bent on getting her? If it wasn't the same guy, she was moving in with me where I knew she'd be safe. Nodding, I escorted her over to the patrol car and tapped on the glass. The scuzz-bucket turned and glared at us, no emotion on his face.

Cass turned away and murmured, "It's him."

"Are you sure?"

"I'm sure. It's the eyes."

"Okay."

Smith walked over saying, "I should go get James."

"NO! I'm fine. I don't want to see him." The three of us were speechless at her words. He had really fucked things up with her. She turned her attention to me, "I assume that's your handiwork on his face?" I just nodded. "I just want to go home."

Cassidy looked to Paul, who seemed hesitant to take her home. She walked away from all of us and headed toward the parking garage. I nodded at Paul and he caught up to her as they disappeared into the garage.

"So, what now?"

Smith asked exactly what I was thinking. "I'm going to follow them down to the station and make sure this gets handled. You going to tell me who your connection is down there?"

"Nope. If I told ya, I'd have to kill ya." He crossed his arms and smiled.

"Alright. I'll be in touch." We shook hands and I walked back to my truck after talking to some of the other officers on the scene.

I got home later than I expected and Jane was getting ready for work. Sitting her down, I told her what happened to Cassidy. "Thank God Paul and Smith were there."

"Tell me about it. I can't think about what could've happened to her."

THE NEXT FRIDAY, Jane and I had Paul and Cassidy over to play cards and eat pizza. Jane had insisted on inviting Cassidy over after I invited Paul.

"Cal, she's all alone. She could use the company."

I knew she was right and just trying to help. It's why I loved her so. Cassidy seemed to have a good time, but she just wasn't herself. She was experiencing heartbreak like I'd never seen and I didn't know how to fix it.

SUNDAY, I MADE plans to have dinner with Cassidy, since Jane had to work. I picked up the Chinese food and made my way to her place. Seeing no other cars there, I used my key and found her curled up on the couch. Her eyes were puffy and her face was tear-streaked.

I sat down next to her and gently asked, "What is it, Cassidy?"

She didn't make a move, just cried, "It's too late. It's over."

"What do you mean, with whom?"

She turned her head toward me and answered, "James. I ended it. The divorce papers are being drawn up."

"Cassidy, I'm so sorry." Maybe it was for the best. If he wasn't willing to be the man my sister deserved, then I didn't want him around. "It's going to be ok."

She didn't eat much and what little she did eat, she puked up. She was so burdened down with emotion that she was making herself ill. She went up to bed as I cleaned the place up and then I headed home.

Easter was the next weekend and we were spending it up at my dad's place. Cassidy was coming too. Family was what she needed.

Easter
~ JANE ~

CASSIDY SEEMED to be in better spirits. Her room was next to the one Cal and I stayed in. I heard her door open and wondered if she was up. My sleep schedule—that was constantly screwed up—had me awake. I found her room empty and made my way downstairs. She was in the kitchen digging through the cupboards.

"Midnight snack?"

She jumped and said, "Sorry. I didn't wake you did I?"

"Nope. I was awake. Working midnights can be a real pain."

"I bet. I'm starving, but nothing sounds good. Damn Lisa and this new diet of hers. Dad has ice cream here somewhere."

I watched her dig through the freezer until she found what she was looking for. She grabbed two spoons and handed me one. We ate and chit chatted about nothing in particular. Her facial expression changed and she ran to the sink and vomited.

Oh, fuck. Cal had mentioned that she was sick last weekend too. The signs were there. Her breasts seemed larger than I remembered, she had been complaining about being bloated. Did she even know or suspect? She rinsed out her mouth and apologized.

"Cassidy?"

Shaking her head she said, "I need to go to the doctor. I feel good for a few days and then I get sick again. I'm beginning to think I have a virus or an ulcer."

"Cassidy!"

"Yes, Jane?" I just looked at her and she was getting a complex as she asked, "Do I have something on my face?"

"When was your last period?" Her eyes got big as the meaning of my words took root. "Are you pregnant?"

"No!" She started looking around the room and said to herself more than to me, "I can't be. I'm on the pill."

"It can still happen."

She walked to the wall calendar and pulled it down. She became panicked as she looked at the month of March and then February, flipping back and forth between the two months.

She looked to me and she was white as a ghost. "I think it was the end of February, maybe early March." She flipped back to April. "I'm never late. Oh, God." She hung the calendar back up and fiddled with keys hanging up and headed toward the door.

"Cassidy, where are you going?"

"I have to know, now."

"It's midnight."

"There's a corner store a few minutes from here that's open twenty-four hours."

"Well, you're not going alone."

She bought the test as the clerk eyed us both curiously. We were both in pajama pants, shirts, and slippers. We drove back to the house and headed up to her room. Everyone seemed to still be asleep. She closed her door and sat on her bed with the test.

"I've never taken one before."

"Really? It's easy."

"Have you?" Nodding, I told her that I was pregnant once, but lost the baby. She didn't need all the horrible details. "I'm sorry." She started crying. "What am I going to do?"

"What do you mean?" Did she not want kids? "Well, I'm guessing if you are, you're around eight weeks, give or take. And you have choices."

"No. If I'm pregnant, I'm keeping it. I could never. But, James will be furious."

"Why would he be furious?" Was she trying to tell me something? I was so confused.

"He had divorce papers drawn up. If I tell him I'm pregnant, he'll think I'm trying to trap him. He doesn't want me. Having a kid won't change that, just complicate everything."

"So, if you are, it's definitely his baby?" She glared at me. "I'm sorry. I had to ask."

She was still crying. "Yes, it's his."

"Hey. Let's take the test before we start trying to figure out the future."

She walked into the bathroom and closed the door. I was waiting for her when Cal walked in.

"What are you two doing up? Everything ok?"

I got up and tried to get him out of the room. "Yes, just some girl talk. I'll only be a few more minutes."

"You're up to something. I can smell it on you."

"Shush before you wake up your dad and Lisa." I pushed him toward our room. "Go." When he walked back in, I went back in to Cassidy's room, closed and locked the door.

I was getting ready to ask her if everything was ok, when she opened the door. With a shaky hand and tears running down her face, she handed me the test. I looked at it and our suspicions were confirmed. She was pregnant. I was going to be an aunt!

I talked with her for a while longer. Eventually she went to sleep and I tiptoed back to bed. I agreed to keep her secret. She needed to see a doctor and talk to James. Cal would blow a gasket for sure. Cal rolled over and pulled me close. I couldn't help the thoughts that danced through my head of our own children. I had a crazy thought about getting pregnant as soon as possible so that Cassidy and I could raise our babies together.

Babies would come. Cal would be a great dad and I couldn't wait to become his wife. I was glad that we decided to marry quickly.

Regardless of all the horrible events we'd all gone through, things were looking up. I could see the sun on the horizon. Thanks to Cal, all my bad memories were fading away.

epilogue

~ JANE ~

I HAD JUST LEFT CASSIDY AT HER place, after her first appointment with her OB. They drew some blood and did a vaginal ultrasound that confirmed she was almost eight weeks pregnant and due in early December. They had her schedule an appointment for a few weeks out to check her progress. There were no issues, though Cassidy was concerned about the stress of her new job.

When we left and got back in the car, she was examining the picture they had printed out for her, but looked sad. I took her hand in mine and gave it a reassuring squeeze.

She squeezed mine back and murmured, "He should be here with me."

"Well, now you can tell him, and you have the proof in your hands."

She started crying, "He's going to hate me."

"Oh, Cassidy. He's not going to hate you. He might be surprised, but he won't hate you."

"You don't understand."

"Understand what?"

She sighed, "I can't get into it, but I said something to prove a point, and I shouldn't have said it."

"We all say things we regret. Apologize to him."

"I wish it was that simple."

"Do you want to stay married?"

She looked at me and without meaning to, I had made it worse. Sobbing, she cried out between shaky breaths, "I don't want to do this alone. I want James to be there with me, to be a father to our baby."

"Honey, he'll be there. He would never falter on his child."

"I know, but what if he doesn't want me anymore?" Taking a deep breath, "I don't want him to stay with me because of the baby."

"James loves you, Cassidy. I know that right now things look like they're doomed, but they're not. You guys created a life. That's a miracle and you did it out of love, whether it was planned or not." She rubbed at her tears and smiled. "Focus on the good. You're going to be fine. Everything will work out." I wanted to believe that Cassidy and James belonged together. Maybe the baby would be the kick in the ass he needed.

She said she was going to call him soon and ask to see him. I promised to keep her news to myself, though I was dying to tell Cal. He'd be upset at first, but I knew that he'd love that baby as much as I would and he'd support Cassidy no matter what.

I WAS HEADED to work several days later when I got a frantic call from James. "Slow down, I can't understand you."

"Cassidy is in the hospital and she'd only let me call you."

"What happened?"

"She was at my place and she fell down the stairs." He was rambling and in a panic. "She was knocked unconscious, but when she woke up she was talking nonsense about a baby."

"James. She's pregnant." There was complete silence on his end. "James, where is she now, where are you?"

"We're at the hospital. They're checking her for a concussion, but she won't let me stay with her. She would only talk to me long enough to ask I call you."

Why wouldn't she let him stay with her? Something else was going on. "Ok. Just calm down. I'll be there soon."

When I got to the hospital, thankful I was early for my shift and had time, I found James and interrogated him further. He didn't reveal anything, or wouldn't. I headed back to see Cassidy and she started crying.

"Cassidy, what happened?"

"I went to his place, to surprise him. Joke's on me. Melissa is staying there. We're not even divorced and he's sleeping with *her*."

"WHAT?" That douchebag. What in the hell was going on? I didn't have a chance to ask any more questions because the attending doctor came in.

"You have a mild concussion, but we're concerned about the spotting. This early in a pregnancy there's nothing we can do to stop it." A nurse brought in an ultrasound machine as Cassidy laid back. "We're going to check and see what's going on." The doctor squirted the jelly on her belly and began looking for the baby. I held her hand, mentally chastising James, as they did the exam. "There's your baby."

Cassidy let out an exasperated breath as James voice filled the small space. "It's true?" He had snuck into the room without any of us knowing. The doctor asked who he was and he replied, "I'm her husband."

When Cassidy confirmed, the doctor reiterated, "This is your baby," and pointed to the screen. He pushed a few buttons and the *whoop, whoop, whoop*, filled the air. I knew what the sound was, but James and Cassidy didn't. "And that is your baby's heartbeat."

James stared at the screen in disbelief as his eyes traveled to Cassidy's belly. I felt like an intruder on this special moment, but witnessing it just confirmed everything. My cousin was desperately in love with Cassidy and I knew that the feeling was mutual.

"I'm going to send you home. Remember to take it easy the next couple of days. If the spotting continues or gets worse, you need to call your doctor. We're treating this as a threatened miscarriage, for now. Good luck."

"Thank you."

They were quick to get her discharged and James offered to take her home. She was still upset with him and I knew they had a lot to discuss. James and I left her to get dressed and I asked to talk to him outside.

When we stepped outside, I cussed him out. "What the fuck is Melissa doing at your place? I swear to God, James."

"NO. She's just staying there, nothing's happening."

"You expect me to believe that shit, let alone Cassidy?"

"YES!"

"You have a lot of explaining to do."

"You son of a bitch." We both turned toward Paul's voice as his fists shoved James back. "She's pregnant! What did you do?"

James shoved him back, yelling, "I didn't do anything. Why are YOU here?"

"She called me crying."

I tried stepping between them. "You guys, stop."

"What's going on?" Cassidy walked up to us with her discharge papers in hand. Paul rushed to her and asked if she was ok.

"Is it even my baby?" Fuck. James went *there*. He was an idiot, but I understood his doubt. Cassidy just stared at him as Paul turned red. "It's good to know I'm not the only one fucking around."

Paul went to move forward and Cassidy grabbed his arm to stop him. "Well, at least we understand each other."

It was like a train wreck that I couldn't avert my eyes from. The three of them stood there, all silently challenging the other. Cassidy's comment didn't help. Had she lied to me? *Was* Paul the father? Did she even know? And why had James said he was fucking around? He'd just told me that he wasn't. James threw his hands in the air and walked away.

I looked at Cassidy and questioned her, "Cassidy, what are you doing?"

"I've told him the truth over and over. I'm done trying to convince him. If he wants Melissa, that's fine. He just admitted he was fucking around. I'll raise this baby alone."

"No you won't." Paul put his arm around her like he was staking his claim.

Cal was going to have a coronary when he found out. Paul and Cassidy left and I pulled out my cell to call James. He had told me he wasn't sleeping with Melissa. He and Cassidy were so stubborn they couldn't see past their own noses.

James didn't answer his phone. I tried calling James for hours. Hours turned into several days and days turned into a week. James had dropped off the radar. Nobody knew where he was and Cassidy tried acting like she didn't care.

In the meantime, I sat Cal down to tell him. I couldn't keep all the secrets anymore and hoped Cassidy would understand.

"Cal, Cassidy's pregnant."

The End

Playlist for Fading Away

Running Up That Hill by Placebo
Dust to Dust by The Civil Wars
Come a Little Closer by Dierks Bentley
Fire It Up by Black Label Society
New Favorite Memory by Brad Paisley
Turning Page by Sleeping At Last
Who I Am With You by Chris Young
Cruise by Florida Georgia Line
Must Be Doin' Somethin' Right by Billy Currington
My Kind of Love by Emeli Sande
More Of You by The Goo Goo Dolls
Don't You Wanna Stay by Jason Aldean & Kelly Clarkson
BulletProofAngel by The Goo Goo Dolls
This Is How We Roll by Florida Georgia Line & Luke Bryan
Dirt Road by Kip Moore
Young Love by Kip Moore
Somethin' 'Bout A Truck by Kip Moore
Beer Money by Kip Moore
Hey Pretty Girl by Kip Moore

More from J.M. Witt

The Anchored Hearts Series
Letting Go (Vol. 1)
Hiding Away (Vol. 1.5)
Letting Go of You (Vol. 2)
Fading Away (Vol. 2.5)
Letting Go of Us (Vol. 3)

The Blind Vows Series
Trust, Honor, Love: (Vol. 1)
Body, Heart, Soul: (Vol. 2)

Woodland Creek Series
Mina's Revenge

KinkyFodder Chronicles
My Secret Submission: (1)
My Secret Possession: (2)

About the Author

Residing in Metro Detroit, International Bestselling Erotic Author J. M. started writing poetry and short stories as a young girl. Rediscovering her love of reading, after having her fourth child, she started writing again. She also works full time as an Office Manager for a large landscaping company.

Letting Go, her first publication, was released in December 2013 and 10th novel was published in January 2017.

She enjoys music, time with friends, sarcasm, concerts, spending time with her children and husband, traveling, and getting lost in a good book.

And if you ask nicely, she might show you her flogger and let you sample it.

Official playlist for Fading Away on Spotify

If you or a loved one has been a victim
of sexual abuse or assault;
There is help for you.
www.rainn.org
1.800.656.HOPE